The Battle of Sleeping Lady

Guardians of Sanctuary Book Three

TL SHIVELY

Acknowledgements

I have never had a desire to see Alaska; it was never once on my bucket list until my dad and stepmom managed to convince me and Paul to spend a week and a half there. They showed us the beauty and peace that was their Alaska. Thank you, Dad and Kay. You gave us an experience that we will never forget and has now become part of the Sanctuary Guardian story!

I would also like to thank the real Drake for giving me the inspiration for my Drake and his big time! Here I thought, "When you don't know what to say you say Supercalifragilisticexpialidocious!" Thanks to Drake, I know it is "Big time!"

- Arions- The inhabitants of Sanctuary
- Blood Crystals- The first crystals that were discovered, they were blood-red in color
- Chenra- A magical metal used by Serdita and her sister Soliel to make music
- Command Center- The military establishment that resides in the mountains that protects Sanctuary
- Crim- Crystals used to enhance the power of an Arion, only the Guardians are able to use their powers without a Crim
- Crystal Essence- The powder from crystals that is highly unstable
- Healers- Arions who use the crystals to heal or do damage control such as adjust someone's memory
- Illusion Crystals- Crystals used to create illusions to help the Arions keep the knowledge of their existence from the world
- Leaders- A group that run the Sanctuary, it should be noted that Arions have never seen any of them
- Magine- A shadow creature created by the Shadow Master, Crims don't affect this creature, only the Guardians can stop it
- Memory Crims- Crystals used in altering someone's memory
- Mythrian Metal- A special metal used in the creation of Crims
- Normies- Mortals who know nothing of the Sanctuary
- Parent Crystals- Large Crystals that are used to give the crystal Crims their power
- Power Ball- A crystal ball used in training one's powers

- Productive Crims- Crystals used in daily life around the Command Center powering computers, opening doors and more
- Rotary- The magical Crim bracelet that was designanted as unstable but now resides on Telara's wrist
- Shadow Generals- More human looking than the minions and bigger in size, they command the minions and only battle when needed by the shadow master
- Shadow Master- The being that controls all the shadows
- Shadow Minions- The lowest ranking of Shadows and also most common, if you were playing chess these would be considered the pawns
- Shadows- Creatures made of shadows commanded by the Shadow Master
- Stargazer- A black slim box resembling a small laptop covered with strange symbols that only I.Q. is able to understand
- Static Room- Room in the Bungalow where the Guardians could relax with their powers

Chapter 1

Breathing hard as a droplet of sweat rolled down her nose before jumping off its bridge and down to the dusty ground beneath her, Telara tried not to roll her eyes at herself for her thoughts about her suicidal sweat drop. For some reason, she was having a feeling of *déjà vu*. It was just a year ago that she and the others had come to Sanctuary thinking it was a summer camp for teenagers. It didn't take them long to realize there was more to this camp than what it was portrayed as. If the fairies, mermaids, and other magical creatures they discovered weren't enough to tell them that their lives had changed, finding out they had powers definitely had.

Telara looked around the training field at the others who were training with the Alpha Faction as well. Their powers were becoming impressive, their control over them even more so. She watched as the grass beneath Gage's feet grew and wrapped around him causing him to trip as Vanna used her staff to vault over him. Vanna, the mother hen of the group, had power over the earth around them and an infinity with the animals that resided within.

Gage, the Alpha second was laying on his back laughing with those blue eyes staring up at Vanna who was grinning down at him, her auburn hair flying around her in the wind. Vanna stood there in her earth-tone-colored clothes and green eyes looking the part of Mother Nature. Alphas normally wore their shiny black suits, but Gage was wearing a white T-shirt and jeans.

Since they were training, the Guardians were dressed in regular street clothes as well rather than their new purple ethereal-looking uniforms as they raced around the training fields with the other Factions of Sanctuary. Well, raced, vaulted, jumped, flipped, and even soared as in Tia's case. Trent, another Alpha, whose dark, black, spiky hair was tinted at the ends with bright green, had attempted to get her in a leg lock, but she took to the air, her winds helping her to soar at least five feet off the ground, her long blond hair billowing out behind her. Tia controlled the element of air and, in the past year, her control over her powers had become so much better.

Chance and Cole worked together when it seemed as if Sapphire and Stella were going to team up against them. Stella, they knew, was almost as formidable an opponent as Pam with her knowledge of weapons and her ability to make her Crim work even better than any of the Guardians. Furthermore, unlike others whose Crim only formed into one weapon, Stella's Crim changed into whatever weapon she was in the mood to wield.

Chance, the captain of the boys' swim team at their school, had brown hair that fell over his forehead. With those hazel eyes of his, he gave one of those smiles that always had the girls at school giggling. As Stella moved stealthily along the ground, the grass beneath her feet became soaked with the water that was rising from the earth. Her feet moved swiftly over the grass until she stepped in a very slippery patch created by the water, she slid and landed with a splash on the ground.

Sapphire managed to flip over her and avoid winding up sprawled on the ground as well. While Stella's long brown hair was in a neat ponytail that was now fanned out over her face, Sapphire's copper red curly hair was flying around her face as she vaulted over the ground. Cole leaned down and stared with great concentration as Sapphire closed in on him. His brown eyes glowed red, and his sandy brown hair stood on end as the air around them grew warmer. Steam slowly started to rise from the ground and then became so thick that it hindered their visibility. Not only that, but the steam frizzed and stuck to Sapphire's face making it even harder for her to see.

While Chance and Cole had them distracted, Chance's twin Chad stood on the outside of the fog. A crackling sound could be heard as four ice walls formed around the fog, rising tall and encasing the two Alphas inside. I.Q. ended up on his ass since he was too busy laughing at the awesome teamwork they had just witnessed. Donny joined his fellow Alphas sneaking up on I.Q. with a smirk and using his baton on the back of I.Q.'s legs.

"Come on Guardian, you know the Shadows will use any means to take you guys down."

The air around them electrified, and Donny ended up with hairs on end before a small (well, Telara hoped it was small) shock sent him on his own rear. It must not have been too bad as Donny's freckled face broke out in a grin as he looked at the dark-haired Guardian.

"Not bad, Oh Voltage One! Now can you tone it down, so I don't look like big foot for my date tonight?" Donny's copper hair looked frizzed out, the hair on his

THE BATTLE OF SLEEPING LADY

head and arms indeed making him look like the legendary hairy big foot.

That brought a round of laughter as they felt the air clear, and Donny was able to calm his hair down some.

"Whoa!"

Telara moved just in time before Pam would've had her laying on her back with some help from her staff. She flipped back and used her power to create a sort of force field around her to block any more blows. They had been out there for hours practicing using their powers, using Crims, and just fighting. You name it, they were practicing it. The Guardians were becoming so proficient with not only their Crims but their powers as well. Telara was feeling pride in her friends and herself.

When they first came here to Sanctuary, they were awkward teenagers with no idea who they actually were. They started out at odds with Pam, the leader of the Alpha Faction, but ended up good friends not only with Pam but also many others here at Sanctuary. The previous Guardians that had come before them had a reputation for being highly antisocial, so when they had arrived, they already had marks against them. It took the disaster of losing Gage to the Shadows before they had all learned to work together. And while they had ended up getting Gage back, there had been a price: Gage could no longer wield his Crim.

A shrill whistle had them stopping and looking to see Raphael walking towards them. Cole melted the ice wall and Vanna called back her roots as they stood up and walked to meet him. School was out, and they were back in Sanctuary for the summer. Training, eating, sleeping, and training, eating, sleeping. You get the picture. Satyrs and gnomes appeared with towels and water for them.

"Getting better," Raphael praised them as he cantered towards them.

Their training with Raphael was now done with different members of the Command Center's forces. Today's training was with the Alpha Faction, while yesterday it had been with the Theta Faction.

Raphael looked at Pam. "Carmen is waiting for you at the Command Center."

Pam groaned; the others didn't blame her when it came to Carmen. The leader of the Beta Faction wasn't very well liked; she tended to treat others as if they were beneath her. They had all been the target of Carmen's ungracious remarks.

"I forgot about the performance evaluations."

"You get to evaluate Carmen?" Cole stared wide eyed at Pam who shook her head.

"No." She sighed. "The leaders of the Factions are evaluated by Ira, but I get the fun job of looking over the leaders' evaluations of their teams. Carmen's is always the most fun." She looked at them, and they could hear the frustration in her voice; they felt bad for her. "You guys wanna join?"

Not that bad though.

They looked at each other, each face a mirror image of the other, causing Pam to laugh at them.

"No worries! This meeting is only for the leaders." She laughed even harder at the look of relief that crossed their faces. "I guess you guys have some free time. I'll see you at dinner."

With a wave, she was gone. The others started to take

off for the showers, not sure what to do with this sudden free time. Raphael stopped them.

"I do believe young Gage might require some assistance if you find yourselves at loose ends."

With that said, he cantered away. They looked at each other and shrugged; it was better than dealing with Carmen.

Entering the Command Center and waving to a white coat who was walking by, Telara stopped to watch her walk causing the others to stop and look at her.

"Do you guys realize I don't think there is one white coat that we know by name?"

"Sure there is," Cole protested. Telara just raised an eyebrow at him. "I think." He looked at the others. "Isn't there?"

They stood there for a few minutes, none of them able to think of one. They had always seemed so nice to them, although Pam did say they didn't have much of a sense of humor.

Vanna just shrugged and started walking away.

"So, we will find a white coat and ask him his name. Problem solved."

They stared at one another. Would she really? They looked back and watched her stop a dark-haired male in a white coat. Yes, yes, she would.

She walked back towards them grinning wide while leaving the poor male staring after her with a very puzzled look on his face. They couldn't blame the guy; Van had a way that no one could ever explain. As she reached them, she gave a very satisfied grin.

"His name is Leo."

The residents of Sanctuary were called Arions, and the ones who worked in the Command Center were usually defined by their wardrobe. The Factions were the protectors of Sanctuary. When they were battling the Shadows, they wore suits that fit like a second skin. Each Faction wore a suit whose color was specific to them. You also had the maintenance workers who wore brown jackets, and the healers of the Command Center who wore white jackets, which was why the Guardians called them "White Coats." This was the first time they knew any of them by name, thanks to Vanna.

Not another word was said as they went in search of Gage. Telara thought about the time since they had left the island. It had been nine months since that day, and they had seen nothing of Kull nor heard anything. When they told Lucius about him, he just smiled and said that he was sure that Kull was thankful for being released from that curse. The curse had kept him imprisoned as a dragon guarding a town that had been cursed by the Gods. If not for them, Kull would still be a dragon stuck in that town.

For the past nine months, they have trained their fighting skills, strengthened their powers, and had tried to live normal lives. All this while constantly looking over their shoulders wondering if some errant God or Goddess wasn't going to pop up and cause them problems. Not to mention wondering why the Shadow attacks had suddenly slowed down. That even had Lucius concerned.

Their powers were coming so much easier to them now. Their Crims were working as if they were now just an extension of themselves. Claw had even come up with a new discovery that made suiting up for battles easier, not just for the Guardians but for all Arions. (Claw was the hot-tempered, red-headed Scotsman and leader of the Gamma Faction. He was always butting heads with Ira, who was head of the Command Center. Claw was also a genius when it came to the crystals.) Now, whenever they needed to suit up in uniform, they just had to think it, and the Crim would suit them up. It made it so that the Sanctuary defense forces didn't have to constantly be wearing their uniforms; they could actually walk around in civilian clothes. Of course, the leather belts still had to be worn; Claw hadn't managed to find a way around that one just yet.

Every time Claw would come out with a new discovery, it would cause many to laugh because Ira would just shake his head and walk away. Of course, Claw would never try to rub Ira's nose in the fact that his discoveries were considered breakthroughs and wanted throughout Sanctuary. At least not daily that is.

Juggling being a normal teenager and a Guardian learning their powers wasn't always easy; they had had a few mishaps over the past nine months. Like when Cole thought Raven's clones were Shadows and brought out his fiery nunchucks. Their hair was singed, and it required bringing in the healers to modify their memory. Also, it brought on a lecture from Ira on keeping their identifies secret.

They found Gage in the detainment barracks where the Shadow creatures were contained until they could be cured. Gage was staring at one of the minions that was climbing the bars of his cell like a monkey. The look on his face had them stopping cold; he was staring at the minion with an almost lost look. There were times they managed to forget that he had been taken and transformed into a minion until that fateful battle where Sanctuary had been attacked, and the damage had taken them months to repair. They couldn't even imagine what he was dealing with.

Not all the Shadows had been able to be cured. Their fate was in the hands of the leaders right now. Ira wanted them to be terminated; his excuse was that keeping them when they can't be cured is dangerous. Lucius argued that they can't be given up on, not only because of the fact that they were possibly fellow comrades but that they were living beings. So, for now, the fate of the uncured Shadows remained in the leaders' hands.

One of them must have made a noise because he turned to look at them.

"Oh, hi guys. Sorry, I was just off in my own little world." He gave a half grin.

Cole just shrugged. "No worries, man. I mean last year you were one of them. Can't expect you to get over it like that." Tia elbowed him. "Ouch…Wha?" He frowned at her. "Not like it isn't common knowledge you know."

This time, she smacked him on the back of his head. "You really need to learn some people skills, you jerk. Have some tact."

Gage laughed. "That's alright; he's right." He looked back at the cages. "Last year, I was one of them. My counselor told me that the best way to get over what happened to me is to talk about it."

"Counselor?" Cole looked at him. "With what happened to you man, they should have given you a shrink. Someone with experience to handle head cases."

Gage stepped in before Tia could seriously hurt Cole who was still oblivious as to why she was getting upset at him. "That is what our counselors do; they are better trained than most of the credited psychologists out in the world. They are just called counselors." He looked back at the minions that were now watching the Guardians with intense stares. "You know, when I was in their shoes, I saw everything."

They looked at each other, suddenly feeling extremely uncomfortable. Every single one of them had been curious about what he had went through, although none had had the courage to ask. Now that he was telling them about it, they kind of felt as if they were intruding.

"It was a weird sensation to be aware of everything and yet unable to do anything. As soon as the Shadow had control of my body on that stone slab, I no longer controlled my actions. I had to watch as he attacked my friends, his only purpose to destroy and capture for his master. It was like I was there, yet not there."

Telara felt a lump in her throat at the sound in his voice; it gave them a different view of the creatures in the cages looking at them. If released, these creatures would capture any of their friends, especially them. Yet, it wasn't the fault of whoever is imprisoned inside the Shadow. Life was so unfair.

A loud growl had them jerking around to face the larger cage on the other side of the room.

"Holy cow! What is that?" Chad stared wide eyed at the dark creature that prowled the cage, reminding them of a large, very large, feline. The eyes were like round orbs of fire.

"We don't know; it took three Factions to capture it. Several ended up in the infirmary." Gage stared at the creature who was looking at them as if they were its next meal. "Another that can't be cured by any Liberator that has been made."

A Liberator Crim was the Crim that had been created from the parent crystal Vanna had given power to after that major battle. The only function for the Crim is to free the Shadow creatures created by the Shadowmaker.

"Hey, Gage! They are waiting for us."

They turned and saw Zeke, the leader of the Theta Faction, standing at the door.

"I'll be right there." Gage turned to look at them. "We have to get supplies to our Sanctuary in Alaska. Want to go with?"

"Alaska!"

They laughed as Van's eyes grew bright; they knew how much she loved Alaska even though she had never been there. She had always said Alaska called to her. Of course, there was a lot more wilderness up there, and she was their Mother Nature.

"That would be a yes." I.Q. grinned.

Chapter 2

"So, did you hear the latest?"

Gage looked over at Zeke and shook his head at the question.

"Looks like Ira might get his way."

This got their attention. If Ira was getting his way on something, it didn't usually bode well for them or their friends. Ira wasn't really a bad guy; he just tended to see things in black and white. They had been stacking boxes of supplies onto the transport platform, getting them ready to go with them to Alaska. They had been super excited about going, but now they were listening to Zeke.

"From what I heard, when the Shadow hound got loose and put that nymph into the med unit, Ira went right to the leaders."

Gage's brow furrowed. "The leaders ordered the hound's execution?" His tone suggested that the fact bothered him. Which they understood; he had been a Shadow at one time. This whole Shadow situation had to be harder on him than anyone. They wondered why Ira couldn't see that.

"No, they're holding out unless Ira can come up with a humane way to put the Shadows down."

"How close is Ira to coming up with it?" I.Q. looked at Zeke.

"Not close but if another Shadow escapes, he might not need it." Gage looked troubled at that thought, and Zeke looked at him. "Sorry, man."

"Not your fault. Ira has a point. It sucks, but he is right. We have to be able to secure the safety of Sanctuary and our people."

"But the Shadows are our people too," Vanna argued. "Well, there is a chance they are but even if they aren't ours, they are still innocent."

Gage gave her a small smile. "I wish it was that simple."

Before they could get deeper into discussion, Claw joined them with a packing list of the supplies they were taking along with instructions.

"Dinnea forget tae meet wi Cecil, he has some new discoveries he was wanting tae show me."

Cole looked at Claw. "Why don't you just go with us and talk to him yourself?"

Claw shrugged. "Let's just say thay dinnea have a sense o' humor." That made them very curious, but he just turned back to Zeke.

"Cecil swears he has some inventions that will make us drool," Zeke said.

Claw looked at the Guardians and grinned. "Enjoy the trip."

With that said, he walked away.

"What's that supposed to mean? They don't have a sense of humor?" Telara was curious now.

"Ummm...let's just say Claw had a disagreement with one of the ruling supernatural families of Alaska," Gage said not looking up from the packing list.

Zeke gave a nasally laugh. "From what I heard the

mermaids were so upset that they refused to enter the mermaid tanks for months after that."

They looked at each other.

"Mermaid tanks?"

They couldn't imagine a mermaid letting anyone keep them in tanks.

"You'll see." Zeke winked at them.

"So, Claw isn't the only crystal specialist?" Vanna asked.

Gage looked up at her and shook his head. "Every Sanctuary has its own crystal specialist. They each have Factions just like us with the same responsibilities, sorta," Gage told them but before they could question him, he continued. "Since the restrictions have been lifted thanks to you guys, new inventions have been coming out from each one. Claw has been in constant communication with the other Sanctuaries."

"There are other Sanctuaries?"

Gage and Zeke looked at each other.

"Of course, there are."

Before they could say anything more, the porter tech interrupted.

"Okay, guys! Let's get this delivery done so we can be back by dinner time."

They nodded as they stepped up on the platform together, putting their glasses on when the porter tech told them to. The bright light surrounded them for a matter of seconds before fading. They were no longer in the Gamma quarters; now, they looked like they were in a cave. The walls around them were stone as was the floor, and the air felt damp.

"Bringing guests this time, Gage?"

They turned from their inspection of the room and saw the source of the feminine voice walking towards them. A brunette whose hair was laying limply around her angular face with big brown eyes was staring at them curiously. She was wearing a white tank top, pink shorts, and purple rubber boots.

"Jess, meet the Guardians."

Jess nodded as Gage introduced each of them to her before turning around and starting to give orders to others (others that they hadn't noticed when they were looking around the cave), telling them to get the supplies checked in and ready for transport to Sanctuary.

"Aren't we at the Sanctuary?" Cole asked the same question that was running through their minds. If this wasn't the Sanctuary, where were they?

"You'll see," Zeke told them with his eyes twinkling in mirth at their confused expressions.

They walked around the cave as the Alaskan Sanctuary workers started going over the packing list with Gage and Zeke.

"Kara said to make sure there was some of Silest's famous brew," a freckled, redhead, very tall, and lanky kid spoke up as he was moving boxes. "The forest nymphs here go nuts for that stuff."

Zeke chuckled. "Yeah, Silest made sure to send some." He looked over at them. "You know you guys can always go topside and check things out while we go through this if you want. We can grab ya before we head down to the Command Center."

"Topside?"

Telara shrugged when Tia looked at her.

"Come on, I'll show ya, but you'll have to suit up;

the bears topside know to leave the Sanctuary workers alone but if you are in civilian gear, they consider you fair game." Jess motioned for them to follow her.

They were staring at each other with wide eyes thinking about bears. Quickly, they pushed the new buttons on their Crims and were suited up within seconds in their purple ethereal fineness.

They followed Jess through a connecting tunnel. Wherever they were, the walls around them and the floor beneath them was stone. They even saw some moss along crevasses in the wall as they did their best to keep up with Jess who was moving along as if the stones weren't slippery. They reached the end of the passageway and saw a rope ladder hanging along the wall in front of them. Jess climbed nimbly up the ladder and opened some type of circular wooden door overhead, motioning for them to follow her through the hatch. Exiting the passageway, the bright light of an Alaskan daytime momentarily blinded them. Looking around their surroundings, they saw trees and stones. Looking down the hill they were standing on, they saw water. Lots of it.

"Prince William Sound." Jess smiled at them as a seagull gave a cry somewhere far off.

"So, when he becomes king will you change it to King William Sound?" Cole said with one of his cocky grins.

"Huh?" Jess looked confused, and they couldn't blame her. Being around Cole most of their lives gave them an advantage in understanding what he was thinking.

"It wasn't named after any royalty that is still alive."

Tia shook her head, and they watched as Jess finally realized what Cole was saying.

"It was actually named after Prince William Henry in 1778, third son to King George the third."

Tia laughed as Cole looked almost crestfallen that his little joke fell very much short. She started walking along a stone trail that weaved between the trees, stopping with a start when a big black bear ambled right in front of her. It turned and lifted its snout into the air, sniffing before huffing at her.

"How rude!"

Telara started laughing as the bear just ambled away. The first time they see a wild bear this close and all Tia says is how rude because it huffed at her.

"Oh, shut up," Tia grumbled causing Telara and the others to laugh harder.

They walked along with Jess who was telling them about the sound of the boats they could hear roaring through the water. They listened as they looked around them at the bright blue sky. There were no power lines above. The mountains around them were covered with snow; yet, the air was warm.

Jess spoke of the glaciers and how there were 150 glaciers in the sound alone. A butterfly fluttered alongside them as they walked, as if walking with them. Tia held out her finger. They watched as it perched on it.

"Interesting fact: butterflies are actually cannibals," Chad told them, walking past Tia. They groaned, but Jess stopped and looked at Chad as if he had lost his mind. "It's true," he told her with a superior grin. She looked at the others as if asking if Chad was mental.

Telara sighed. "Chad got a useless facts book for

Christmas from an uncle whose sense of humor is just as warped."

Chad turned, giving her an affronted look. "Warped? Uncle Leroy isn't warped."

"He does wear swim fins to Thanksgiving," Chance pointed out, which had his brother frowning at him.

"That doesn't make him warped!" Chad defended.

"His sense of humor, not him," Tia told him.

"Can't you just smell that?" Vanna said, interrupting them before their discussion could turn heated. She lifted her nose to the air and breathed in deep. When it came to Cole, no one wanted a discussion to get heated.

"Sorry."

Chad grimaced while his brother gave him a disgusted look. I.Q. just shook his head while Cole smirked.

Vanna glared at him. "Not that! The air. It smells so crisp and clean. The smell of Mother Nature."

"Crisp? How is air crisp? I want to know," Chad said making sure to keep a good distance from Vanna, almost dancing around her. "Potato chips are crisp, but air? And wait a minute! Aren't you Mother Nature?"

They laughed when Chad took a nosedive into a mud puddle from a root that just mysteriously grew up and tripped him.

"Hey! Foul play!"

Jess quickly started talking about all the animals that inhabited the sound and its many islands: bears, otters, eagles, porpoises, whales, and even foxes.

"Foxes?" Telara looked over at Jess while the others laughed. Telara and her love of foxes was well known, as well as her hatred of spiders.

"Yes, at one time there were 34 islands in the sound

that had fox farms. Being on an island helped prevent the animals from running away. The last one closed in 1959, I believe."

"What exactly did they farm the foxes for?" Telara frowned.

"Don't answer that!" Cole warned Jess who had been about to open her mouth to answer.

His eyes darted to Vanna before looking back at Jess. Jess looked over at Vanna whose face was scrunched up and whose eyes were narrowed. Something in those wrinkles must have given Jess the clue as to what Cole was trying to warn her of. Instead of talking about fox fur, she turned around and began walking away telling them about Whittier, the town that was known as the gateway to Prince William Sound.

Vanna looked as if she were about to interrupt Jess. They were sure it was to ask what she was going to say, but the guys were interested in the long tunnel Jess spoke of that the cars had to share with the train. They were bombarding Jess with questions leaving Vanna looking disgruntled.

"Over two miles long!" Chance grinned. "So, has there ever been a car that broke down in the middle of the tunnel?"

Telara didn't hear Jess's reply. While she had paused to process the information regarding the fox farm, the others kept walking and were now out of ear shot. She knew she should probably catch up to them, but she wasn't so sure she wanted to hear more about this place.

She watched as the other Guardians kept walking, their ethereal purple suits a big contrast against the trees and rocks around them. Jess's own suit seemed to work as camouflage with her surroundings as it was constantly changing. She wondered if that was common among the Factions here in Alaska; she was curious about the differences between the Factions.

She had started moving slowly forward when a faint sound of musical notes filled the air. Stepping off the path, she started towards the musical sound as musical notes that seemed to fill the air started to surround her. Literally. The air around her became filled with silver flowing musical notes the closer she got to the music. The temptation to reach out and touch one of the notes was too powerful to resist. As soon as her finger touched one of the notes, it popped as if it were one of the soapy bubbles they used to blow into the wind as children.

Following the silver floating notes through the trees, she found herself on top of the island overlooking the other side. There in front of her, playing a silver fiddle that looked as if it was creating the silver floating music notes floating in the air, was a very limber female dancing around. Telara watched the female, admiring how graceful she moved all while playing that fiddle and not missing a note. Well, not that Telara could tell; the music sounded flawless to her ears.

Her smile became a laugh as a few of the notes swirled around her head. Telara noticed that the silver notes seeming to be fluid and in motion, unlike the one that had popped from her touch earlier. This time, when one of the notes floated in front of her, she saw her friends walking along the path with Jess. Gasping, she caught the attention of the dancing female who turned but never stopped moving or playing her fiddle. Purple eyes stared at her from beneath wild hair floating around a cherub face that changed color in time with the music being played.

"What are you doing here?"

The voice sounded so sweet and flowed as if she was singing along with the music that was playing.

"My name is Telara. Yours?"

The female danced around her still playing the silver fiddle. "I am called Soliel. I know who you are. That isn't what I asked; I asked what you are doing here."

That name sounded so familiar to Telara. Wait! "You are Serdita's sister." Soliel gave a bow without stopping playing the silver fiddle, and Telara gasped. "Is that your Chenra?"

Again, Soliel nodded as she twisted and turned, still playing the fiddle as more silver notes appeared.

"Didn't know they could take the shape of instruments."

This time, Soliel responded although she didn't stop playing. "A Chenra takes whatever shape that its holder desires. Serdita's Chenra doesn't take any shape 'cause she likes variety. To create that variety, the Chenra needs to preserve itself in its natural form."

"Well, it's nice to meet you, Soliel." Telara smiled at her and to her surprise Soliel stopped. Then another surprise (well, not too surprising considering all that Telara had learned in the past year) but still a surprise: The bow in Soliel's right hand melted and slithered up her arm banding around and becoming an arm band. The violin wrapped her left arm before blending in with her skin. They both became tattoos of music notes.

Soliel's comment about knowing who she was finally registered. Telara had been so excited about Soliel's Chenra that at first it didn't register with her.

"What do you mean, you know who I am?"

"You are a Guardian, are you not?"

Telara nodded at Soliel who then moved with ease and grace to walk around her, looking her over.

"Umm…"

"Everyone who is anyone knows who the Guardians are." Soliel paused in front of her, and Telara gasped as she watched her eyes go completely silver. "Except for the Guardians themselves." Her voice seemed to echo around Telara as she spoke, her words sending chills down Telara's spine. "The Guardians are being lied to, and if they have any hope of staying alive then they must discover the truth."

Telara's brow furrowed. She opened her mouth to ask Soliel what she was talking about, but her friends hollering her name stopped her.

She turned around and hollered, "I'm over here."

When she turned back around, Soliel was gone. "Where did she go?"

"Where did who go?" I.Q. appeared at her side; the others were further down the hill waiting on them. They weren't looking very patient either.

Telara opened her mouth but then sighed. "Never mind."

I.Q. shrugged. "Okay, well Gage and Zeke are done and heading to the Command Center with the supplies we brought. They said we will want to see it."

Telara gave one last look around the mountain but still no Soliel. With a shrug, she followed I.Q. down the mountain to the wooden hatch.

Chapter 3

They followed Jess down several tunnels inside the island. The air around them was getting cooler the further down they went.

Chance ran his hand along the walls, feeling the water that surrounded the island.

"We are under sea level."

"Of course we are." Jess smiled. "Where do you think our Command Center is?"

I.Q. suddenly stopped. "In an island?"

The cavern filled with the musical laughter of Jess's voice. "There isn't an island in the sound that is big enough to house the Command Center. Only our receiving department and the homes of the mythicals are housed in and on the islands."

"So where is the Command Center?" Telara cocked her head looking at Jess while I.Q. just stared straight forward with pursed lips as they walked.

Jess gave a sly smile. "You will see."

They arrived in a cavern where Gage and Zeke were waiting for them. As they entered the room, the grin Gage gave them had them looking just a tad nervous. He gripped a handle on what looked like a large, ornate, metal disk on the stone floor. As they watched him lift the disk, they saw it was hinged and when they peered down, they saw water flowing underneath them.

"Whoa!" I.Q. jumped back blinking at the water, his whole body still.

"Static!" Chance grinned down at the water in the hole. He turned back to grin at Jess who was watching them with an amused expression. "Are we doing down there in the water?"

At Jess's nod, I.Q.'s face grew very pale, not that Telara could blame him; electricity and water didn't really mix.

"The Command Center is down there?" Cole was looking down into the hole, his eyes squinting as if he was expecting to see the Command Center from where he was standing.

"It's actually on the floor of the sound," Zeke told them, his eyes sparkling full of mirth as their eyes grew wider than they already were.

Chance was the only one who looked excited about the fact that they would be going down into the water to see the Command Center. Of course, he also could live in the water. The rest of them could swim, but the thought of diving down into the water had them very leery.

"Your suits will protect you," Gage said, finally taking pity on them. "Even yours, I.Q."

"You'll see," Zeke tried to reassure I.Q. who wasn't looking appeased by Gage's statement.

Zeke pushed a button, and his Golden suit appeared. He reached over and pushed a button on the silver bracelet that they hadn't noticed on Gage's wrist. His black Alpha suit encased his body except for his head. With a quick wink, Zeke gave a shrug.

"Always a way around things." As soon as those words left his mouth, Zeke jumped into the hole along with Gage who motioned for them to follow.

⊗ℱ⍳⊛

"They're kidding right?" I.Q. looked at Telara who was staring down into the hole where Gage and Zeke had disappeared. Gage's head broke the water, looking as dry as if he were sitting on one of the benches across form them.

"Come on in, guys! The water is just fine."

With a wink and a beckoning wave, he dove back under the water. I.Q. looked over at a very amused looking Jess.

"The mighty Guardians are scared of a little water?"

They could see the teasing glint in Jess's eyes, but it still had the affect she wanted as Chance just gave a cocky salute before he seemed to just fall into the hole, causing water to splash up on the stone floor.

"As if that is very comforting," I.Q. muttered stepping back quickly and looking at the water as if it were a snake poised to strike.

"Cowabunga!" Cole ran, doing a cannon ball into the water. If Telara hadn't put up a force field, they would have all been soaked. Unfortunately, she wasn't prepared for Chad who followed suit. She glared through the wet bangs hanging down in front of her eyes.

Vanna gave a shrug, walked forward, and stopped right at the edge of the hole. She plugged her nose before jumping feet first right in. Tia, for some reason, wanted to show off. She rose up in the air on a gust of wind, hovering just briefly before the opening where she did a perfect dive into the water. Now, only I.Q. and Telara stood there. Telara didn't want to leave I.Q. standing there by himself as she could feel his reluctance.

Come on guys! Cole said through their mental link. This is static! Now I know how Chance feels. A snort could be heard from Chance.

We can breathe under the water, Vanna's voice came through just as excited as Cole's.

Telara grabbed I.Q.'s hand giving him a reassuring smile. "Together?" I.Q. gave a nervous grin, and together they walked to the water jumping in feet first.

Telara flinched as she had expected to feel as if she had jumped into a glass of ice water. Instead, it felt warm and toasty. She opened her eyes looking around at her friends who were grinning at her.

Hey, Telly.

She jolted at hearing Gage's voice in her head; she had never heard his voice in her head before and couldn't help but wonder if he could now read her mind like her friends.

Tia laughed in her head. He can't read our minds and can only hear when we project our words to him. He said it is one of Claw's new additions to our suits.

Hi. Gage nodded to Tia, indicating he heard her, and she couldn't help but grin. Tia nodded her head towards I.Q. who was floating next to them with his eyes squished shut.

I.Q.!!!!

He opened his eyes at Cole's shout in his head, and the amazement showed on his face as he realized he could see underwater, breathe underwater, and speak to them underwater. Most importantly, his powers weren't electrocuting them.

They looked around at the different types of fishes that were swimming by. Vanna reached out to run her hands along the back of a very flat looking fish as if it was a pet.

Halibut, she told them.

I heard they were good eating.

Cole shrugged when they looked at him, then let out a soundless scream as seaweed wrapped around his ankle and pulled him down.

Van!

Telara groaned, but all Vanna did was give a small shrug of one shoulder.

Not funny, Vanna. Cole was glaring as he swam back towards her. Vanna just smirked at him turning to look at Gage and Zeke who were treading water as they listened to their interaction with smiles on their faces.

Are they always like this? Zeke looked at Gage.

Gage's mouth turned up into a grin. You haven't seen anything yet.

Telara's face scrunched up at his words but before she could respond, Gage's laughter filled their heads.

You guys ready?

Telara rolled her eyes before nodding at him; she knew he was having fun at their expense. Not that she could really argue with him anyways; they did tend to poke each other more than they probably should considering their situation with the Shadowmaster and his minions. Then again, it was better to joke and play than let it pull you down in despair.

Follow us.

Gage and Zeke dove down with the Guardians attempting to follow them while trying to not get distracted by all the fish around them. Telara was sure by the time they got to the Command Center the fish around them would already have names.

Vanna gave her a hard stare letting her know that she heard those thoughts and didn't much care for them.

"Wow!" Chance breathed, echoing what was in all of their minds as they looked around the Alaskan Command Center.

They had swum for almost half an hour before they had reached a crystal tunnel below the island. Following Gage inside, they found themselves in an exceptionally large tunnel slide that ended with them splashing harmlessly in a small pool that led into the Alaskan Sanctuary. Here they now stood, staring around and probably looking like tourists.

Unlike their Command Center where the walls were all white and more military like, this Command Center looked like it had just popped out of a fantasy/Sci-Fi novel. The Command Center was underneath a huge glass dome that they were assured was protected by the magic of the crystals that were mined on the sound floor. Most of the interior walls along the hallways were only about six feet high. They were filled with water and contained fish that were swimming along beside them.

The floor was coral. The coral ran up the glass walls approximately six inches, creating a coral base around the half walls where the fish swam. A worker walked up to a wall ahead of them. He grasped a crystal on the wall where an archway appeared in the aquarium-like wall, creating a glass arch which the worker walked through.

That wasn't the only difference they saw; the worker

was in civilian clothes. His shirt was flannel and tucked into his jeans, and he had rubber boots on his feet. The wall went back to the six-foot aquarium as soon as he passed through.

"Did you see that?" Chad asked tightly grabbing I.Q.'s arm.

Jerking out of his grasp, I.Q. rubbed his arm, frowning at Chad. "We all saw it, man. Chill out."

"Why aren't they wearing colored coats?" Tia whispered.

"You will find that we're very laid back here in Alaska."

They turned around to see a guy in a red flannel shirt that was tucked into his jeans watching them with a kind smile. He had white wavy hair with dark streaks that looked as if he had walked out of a wind tunnel and dark stubble peppering his jawline.

Not bad looking for an old guy. Telara tried not to smile at Tia's comment. Cole, on the other hand, threw a dirty look her way. Talk about role reversal.

"Kayne." Gage nodded grasping the man's hand in a very firm handshake. Turning to them, he made the introductions. "Kayne is the head of this Command Center. Kane, these are the Guardians."

They nodded at the introductions, looking Kayne over and noting the differences between him and Ira as well as Lucius.

"It's an honor." His smile seemed genuine, and his voice was friendly. "You will find that we don't stand on ceremony here." He looked back at Gage. "Have you showed them around?"

"Was about to do that. You want to join us?"

"Would love to." Kayne turned and started down the hallway.

Big difference than Ira, Cole said, his voice full of laughter. They had to agree with him.

They followed Kayne, listening as he told them about the Command Center and how it expanded out over the entire sound floor.

"The entire sound?" I.Q.'s eyes grew wide.

Kayne nodded. "Yes, there is no way to see all of the Command Center in one day, even on a hover bike. There are places here that I haven't even stepped a foot into."

"Hover bike?" Cole's eyes lit up.

"That you can't ride without a license."

Cole's excitement fell to a crestfallen look that caused them to laugh.

"I would advise you to be careful; you can get lost for days here," Kayne cautioned them.

"Didn't you have one of your Arions disappear for over a week?" Zeke asked, a twinkle in his eyes.

Kayne just shook his head. "There is a big difference between disappearing and hiding out."

Gage and Zeke laughed, but the Guardians' laughter sounded weak even to their own ears.

"Whoa!" Chad backed right into Tia who shoved him forward.

"What is your problem?" she said through her teeth but stopped as she realized what had caused him to stop so suddenly.

"I think I startled him."

They turned around. Inside the aquarium wall, her tail swishing in the water while her arms were leaned on the top of the wall, they saw a blue-haired mermaid. Not only was her hair blue, but her skin was as well. It was bluish with some green that glistened along her body. Her skin resembled the blue leather jacket that Telara had hanging up in her closet at home.

Kayne grinned at their expressions. "Haven't you seen a mermaid before? Didn't you meet Brom?"

"Yeah, we met Brom. But she was in the pond not in the wall," Chad said still staring.

"Not to mention that Brom's skin looks normal... Ouch!" Cole grabbed his arm where Tia, frowning at him, had just pinched it.

"Why do you think they have the walls like that?" Zeke asked, quickly maneuvering Cole away from the wall.

"Because they like fish." Chad shrugged.

His brother shoved at him calling him an idiot. Telara stood between the two before it got too bad and extended her hand towards the blue-haired mermaid.

"Hello! My name's Telara."

The hand that gripped hers was cool to the touch, not to mention very wet.

"I know," the mermaid said with a smile on her face as she looked at Telara. "Even up here in the last frontier we know of the Guardians." Her head tilted looking at Chance. "My cousin Brom told me about you." The glint in her eyes and the way too feline purr in her voice had Chance shifting very uncomfortably from foot to foot.

"Briny." Kayne looked at the mermaid who just grinned before diving back into the water. They jumped back as water splashed over the side of the walls as she swam away.

"Look!"

Vanna pointed to the floor where the water was disappearing. Kayne nodded.

"The floor will soak up the water; otherwise, there would be so many slips thanks to our aquatic friends that like to visit."

"Yeah. So far, we are 30 days without any safety violations."

Standing there in jeans and a button-down black flannel shirt was a guy with dark hair who couldn't be more than eighteen.

"Cecil." Zeke nodded at him making the introductions. "Cecil here is in charge of the Gamma Faction."

They shook hands and greeted him before Zeke told them he would catch up with them later. He wanted to go over some of the new additions that Claw had sent for Cecil.

The Alaskan Command Center was nothing short of a magical wonderland. Briny wasn't the only mermaid they saw. One was a male who was wearing several starfish around his brow and an algae-looking cape floating around him. He also had seaweed necklaces with barnacles attached for decoration around his neck. His skin was a dull green while his hair was oily black and looked very unkempt, which was odd considering mermaids' hair in the water usually looked so flowing.

"Looks like a homemade crown," Cole snickered about the starfish.

Kayne sighed. "Unfortunately, that's exactly what it is."

"Wait!" Vanna stopped and looked at Kayne. "He is royalty?"

Man, they set their standards low. Even Tia couldn't argue with Cole which was saying a lot. The male mermaid they saw looked as if he had a few screws loose, or seashells in his case.

Kayne shook his head. "He thinks he is and since he is harmless the other mermaids let him think that." He sighed. "While he is harmless that doesn't make him any less annoying when he comes into the Command Center demanding that everyone bow to him."

Cole and Chad both snickered.

"Laugh it up," Kayne told them as he opened the door to the command room. "But while many mermaids can sing, his singing sounds like nails on a chalkboard." They shivered at that description. "Exactly."

"Static!" Cole breathed.

That was one way to put it. Their command room was another magical journey. The walls were glass, so you could see the water all around them teaming with sea life. There were no half walls here. There in the distance...was that a castle? A coral crystal with colorful lights lighting up the building as well as the smaller coral buildings surrounding the palace.

"The royal palace," a feminine voice said.

"Hello, Shayne." Kayne grinned at the very regal looking woman who walked up to them, her ebony hair flowing down past her back. She nodded at him then, turning towards them, her eyes filled with curiosity.

"Are these the Guardians that the whole center has been buzzing about?" Her voice sounded very serene, almost monotone with a very slight sound of interest.

Her voice reminded them of royalty, in fact. Her smile was very practiced, and her clothes looked nothing like the others. Her black slacks fit like a second skin, and her shirt was beige silk that flowed with every move she took.

Okay, everyone else looks like they come from the backwoods while she looks like she just walked off of fifth avenue. Telara had to agree with Tia as they just stared at Shayne. Those are Jimmy Choos.

Jimmy Choos?

Her pumps.

Telara tried not to smirk since they were mind speaking and knew from Pam how it bothered others when they did that. Cole's eyes narrowed at them, but he said nothing more. Kayne didn't seem to find Shayne's attire to be out of place as he did the introductions.

"Shayne meet the Guardians: Telara, Tia, Savanna, Cole, Chad, Chance, and I.Q." Shayne nodded to each of them with a regal tilt of her head while holding out her perfectly manicured hand.

Cole practically leaped forward to take her hand and kissed the back of it. The others just stared as Cole looked up at her with star-struck eyes as if he had just seen an A-lister celebrity.

Tia grabbed him by the back of his shirt, pulling him away and giving him a dirty look. He just shrugged grinning at Shayne who didn't look fazed one bit. Shayne just watched them saying nothing.

"Nice to meet you, Shayne." Telara said before Cole could make any more of a fool out of himself or before Tia decided to send him to the ceiling to cool off.

Shayne nodded at Telara, but it was Kayne who answered. "Shayne is the Beta group leader. Here, the Beta group is the one who coordinates all the groups."

"Isn't that what the Alpha group does?"

Kayne grinned at Chad. "The Alpha group and the Theta group work together for the protection of our lands. The Beta group is our administration group; they pretty much run everything from the Command Center. Gamma and Omega are our weapon and crystal specialists while Delta hold the highest honor."

Tia nudged Telara motioning towards Shayne who gave a dramatic eye roll when Kayne mentioned the Theta group.

"Highest honor?" Vanna queried, and they were astonished at the snort they heard from Shayne. It was very low and of course it sounded like a dignified snort, but it was still a snort.

"Our Delta group are our trackers and here in Alaska that is the highest honor," Kayne told them. He didn't seem to notice the eye rolls or the dignified snort of Shayne's or else he just chose to ignore it.

Wow, big difference from the Sanctuary we are from. Everyone has a role here.

And they work together rather than separate. Chad agreed with his brother.

Kayne turned to Shayne. "Have you given the Alpha and Theta groups their orders?"

"Of course." It was clear from Shayne's tone of voice that she was irritated that he even asked her that.

"Yes, she did, but we decided to see if the Guardians might want to go with us, so we waited."

Looking to the other side of the room, they saw several teens with big grins looking at them. Some were standing, some were leaning against the wall, and the others were sitting on the half wall that separated some of the workstations. The half walls were not made out of glass and had no fish or mermaids swimming within.

Chapter 4

"What is that?" Cole pointed to a building just past the railroad tracks. A very large building. Larger than any hotel they had ever seen.

"That is the Buckner Building," Brandon, the Alpha's second-in-command, told them. He reminded Telara of a shaggy dog with his brown hair that needed groomed badly and a big goofy grin that was contagious.

They had just walked out of the transport they used to get from the bottom of the sound to the town of Whittier. Chance wanted them to swim, but Kayne said they were so far out it would take them days to get to the town. The transport was pretty much the same as at home: step on a pad or into a room, bright light almost blinds you if you forget your shades, and then you end up somewhere else. The only difference was the transport they just stepped off of was inside a big shell that rested just on the shoreline outside of Whittier.

Van made a crack about feeling like Aphrodite which caused the Guardians to pause briefly and give the shell platform some uneasy glances. After all, while that comment may have sounded harmless over a year ago, now it reminded them of their time on the cursed island.

The Alpha and Theta Factions had asked if they wanted to go on patrol with them. They couldn't turn down the opportunity to do a patrol in Alaska. The best part?

They were able to wear civilian clothes; jeans, T-shirts, and sneakers made them feel more normal until one of the Thetas just smirked with a twinkle in his eye when they spoke their thoughts out loud.

Telara turned on him, her hands on her hips. "What is that grin for?"

The dark-haired Theta turned and looked down at her, making her feel very small. The man was either a linebacker for the football team or, considering they were in Alaska, he could be a lumber jack.

Great, Telly. You have to pick the biggest one to challenge, Cole's pained voice echoed in her head while the others watched the exchange with wary glances; however, Telara could feel their agreement with Cole. She had been told her whole life that her mouth would get her into trouble.

"Good thing it's summer," he told her watching her with those dark unreadable eyes. His lips still twitched beneath his dark mustache.

"Why?" Telara's expression softened as his words confused her.

"Because you look like a tourist, so you'll fit right in. Alaskans mostly try to ignore tourists, which will work out for us," the giant said before turning around and walking away, leaving Telara standing there with her brow creased.

"What Wes is trying to say, without saying it, is that you will see Alaskans in our favorite rubber boots more than you will sneakers," Lyla, the mousy brown-haired Theta leader, told them with a kind smile.

"The Buckner building was built back in the 1950's by the military," Brandon interrupted them when he noticed Telara opened her mouth to respond.

"So, it is a military building?" Cole looked over at it with interest.

"It was called the city under one roof because the mess hall, sleeping quarters, medical rooms, and all offices were in that one building," Nat, another Alpha who had a very welcoming smile, told them. Nat and Lana both looked as if they could be related; they both had brown curly hair with golden highlights and pale skin.

"Can we check it out?"

Tia grabbed Cole by his collar and pulled him away as he started towards the Buckner building.

Jana's (the Theta second with red spiky hair) shoulders shook with her barely restrained mirth. "It was abandoned by the Army after the 1964 earthquakes. Since then, the interior has deteriorated badly so probably not a good idea."

Walking along the railroad tracks, they noticed there were vehicles that were all in a line by a light as if waiting to enter the tunnel. It seemed as if the cars had been sitting there since they had stepped off the shell platform.

"That is one long light." No longer curious about the Buckner building, Cole was now staring at the cars.

"Why are they just sitting there?" Chance frowned looking at the cars as well.

"Watch." Jana's lips twitched. As they watched, cars came out from the tunnel. "The tunnel is only a single lane, so each side has to wait. Usually, they go every half hour."

"Don't forget how the cars have to wait if the train is coming through," Dale, an Alpha with light hair that went just past his collar, pointed out.

Jana gave a nod.

"So, we have to wait?" Chad frowned at the thought looking around.

"Of course not." Cameron, the Alpha leader, grinned. He walked past the cars that waited in line leaving them no other option than to follow. Of course, since the other Alaskan Arions were following him as well, that was another reason they followed the short dark-haired Alpha leader who strutted past the cars.

When they reached the same mountain that the tunnel ran through, they watched as Cameron reached out and grasped a crystal knob that lit up at his touch. A door in the mountain opened up and as they walked into the room, they saw Jess standing there watching them.

"Ready?"

They looked at each other at Jess's question then over at the grinning Alpha and Theta leaders. Lyla stepped up onto a platform with a nod at Jess. Lyla had an air of confidence with each movement. It was something they saw in Pam and other Arions back home: confidence that seemed to come easy to others but never to them. They were supposed to be the Guardians, the protectors of magic and the world, but no matter how hard they tried, they still felt just like high school students blundering through each day.

With a deep breath, they stepped up on the platform. They looked around, but no one handed them any shades. They stood there and then gasped as glass walls rose around them, curving until they found themselves within a clear sphere-like container. They touched the walls and looked at each other, a little unsure and wondering what was about to happen.

Is the floor going to open up and shoot us to our destination?

That would be so cool.

Better than any roller coaster ride.

"Look." Van interrupted Cole's, Chance's, and Chad's mind speaking excitement. She was pointing above them. Looking up, they saw the stone ceiling opening up. They felt themselves rise above the ground, causing them to brace themselves against the glass wall.

They were in the bubble with the Theta Faction who weren't even trying to hide their amusement. Looking to their right was the Alpha Faction standing calmly in their own bubble with Gage who gave them a wink.

"A little warning would've been nice," Cole groused not moving from where he was braced against the wall. None of them did.

The bubble rose slowly into the air bringing them up over the mountain. Looking down, they could still see the lines of cars waiting for their turn to get through the tunnel. Turning around, they saw the boat docks and laughed as they saw a cruise ship docking.

"Can they see us?" Telara looked at Lyla who seemed more interested in their reactions than the view around them. Of course, it probably wasn't anything new to her.

"No, the bulbs are created out of illusion crystals, so no one sees us unless we want them to."

"Static!"

The others had to agree with Chad on that one; this was pretty static. The bulb floated for just a few seconds. Telara was pretty sure they were doing that so that the Guardians could enjoy the view for a bit longer. Then they started flying through the sky as they watched the view around them changing.

There were mountains everywhere they looked, not to mention glaciers. Glaciers in summertime? They looked at each other but decided to not ask. They decided they acted enough like tourists although they were sure they were seeing a lot more than the average tourist. They looked down at a highway that Lyla told them was considered one the most dangerous roads in Alaska.

"Highway One."

"One?"

"Alaska doesn't have that many highways," Jana told them with a slight lift of her shoulder. "This isn't the U.S. where you have more blacktop than nature."

"Look at that."

They looked down at the water below them along the highway.

"You have to walk out quite a way before you actually get to the water," Chance said pointing out the black looking beach between the highway and the water.

"That wouldn't be a good idea," Lyla told them.

"Not unless you are wanting to commit suicide," Wes told them running his hands through his dark locks. They weren't sure how old he was. Not only did he have a mustache, but he also had a goatee. Along with the body of a quarterback, he also had the smile of a player.

"What do you mean?" Tia looked up at him; she had to since he practically towered over her. He had to be at least 6'4".

"That glacier silt that's there is worse than quicksand," Lyla told them. "There's a story of a married couple who had walked on the silt since it was so firm. The wife wandered out farther than the husband and as he watched, she started to sink. They had a helicopter flown

41

in to pull her out. Let's just say it wasn't a pretty sight."

She wouldn't look at them, but Wes made a gesture of being pulled apart. They felt sick to their stomachs and agreed they would stay far away from that stuff.

"Is it just along this highway?" Vanna asked, her face a bit whiter after hearing that story.

"It is glacier silt," Wes told her. "You need to be careful no matter where you are. Tourists are discouraged from sightseeing without a local."

"Of course, the Guardians could probably walk right on top of the silt without sinking." Jana winked at them.

Don't even think about it, Cole, Tia growled silently through their mind speak.

Telara groaned when she could hear Cole's thoughts about wondering if he could put a fire barrier between him and the silt. Mainly to impress the girls here in Sanctuary, of course.

It was just an idea, Cole bellyached silently glaring at them.

"Welcome to Wasilla," Lyla told them as their bulbs landed behind a large building in some woods. Looking around all they could see was the building in front of them and trees.

"This way."

The Guardians followed the Alaskan Arions and Gage into a building in which there were four-wheelers.

"Are we driving these?"

The Guardians laughed as Vanna was the one who was getting excited. Telara couldn't blame her; she was liking the idea of driving the four-wheelers as well.

Cameron grinned at her enthusiasm and tossed them each a set of keys.

Each had one of their own four-wheelers to drive. Of course, Chad and Cole were so busy trying to race each other that they missed a turn and almost ran into a mother moose with her baby. They were so scared, they screamed and actually jumped off their four-wheelers, running into a nearby tool shed.

Cameron managed to get the mother calmed down and shooed away before joshing the boys who were peeking out through the small window in the shed.

"Is that beast gone?" Cole's shaking voice asked.

"The big bad beast is gone with her baby," Tia teased them; Cole glared at her. "Well, you were on four-wheelers, and you jump off to run into a shed?"

"Actually, there was always a chance of the moose catching them off the wheelers with her antlers," Cameron laughed.

"The best thing they could have done was to run around a tree," Lyla told them. "Moose are not able to do a turn that quickly, so remember that next time."

"Next time?" Chad's eyes grew large.

"You are in Alaska, man," Gage laughed; the others laughed although the Guardians' laughter was a bit nervous.

"Time to head to Darrold's." Brandon revved his four-wheeler.

"Yeah, this time don't argue with Nikos," Lyla snickered as she started down the dirt track. Brandon snorted and muttered something they couldn't hear.

"Let's go." Gage winked at them as they took off down the tracks. They came out to a paved road only to turn down a gravel road.

Wonder who this Darrold guy is?

Telara was just as curious as I.Q. who had been mostly quiet since arriving in Alaska. They were very awed by what they were seeing and feeling.

Don't forget Nikos, Vanna told them.

Only one way to find out.

They nodded in agreement with Telara.

"I am a platinum member! What are you going to do about it?"

Nikos, the colorful bird, kept squawking the same thing over and over again, with a few crazy orders thrown in such as demanding rose petals in the bath and all appliances no more than three feet off the ground. Darrold was a spry elderly woman whose attitude and energies belied her grey hair. She was wearing grey sweats, a pink sweater, and a necklace with a crystal green cylinder charm.

Cameron told them that Darrold was a bit of an eccentric who was also loved by everyone at Sanctuary.

"She definitely has a very extraordinary taste in decorations." Tia grinned looking around the yard where bowling balls were mounted on pillars and bed rails were planted in flower beds with little wooden signs detailing what was planted there.

"Look over there."

I.Q. was pointing back towards the road where they saw some satellite dishes off to the side of the driveway trailing down the hill to a pond at the bottom. Water trickled from dish to dish all the way to the pond where ceramic frogs sunbathed on the shore.

There were lawn decorations all over that were made from odds and ends. On a nearby pole, they saw bicycle seats with handlebars made to look like skull and antlers. Cole pointed out a painted rock that said, "Turn me over." When he turned it over, they barked with laughter. It said, "Now you are taking directions from a rock."

Vanna was running her hands along the trunk of a tree that stood in the front of Darrold's home; its leaves were oddly shaped, almost cylindrical. It fit right in with all the other oddities around them.

"New recruits, Cam?" Darrold looked at the Alpha leader who shook his head.

"They are the Guardians, Darrold."

"Wait!" Chad looked Darrold over. Nikos had settled on her shoulder and was looking them over. "She's human? I didn't think humans were allowed to know about the Sanctuary or Guardians."

They were all curious about that as well since the Alpha and Theta team seemed to be speaking very freely around her. It was Wes who answered him.

"Darrold isn't just a normal human."

They looked at her but couldn't see any wings, tails, or anything that made them think she was a magical creature.

Think she could be a Goddess?

Telara groaned. I hope not.

They were all in agreement with that thought. Their only contact with any type of Gods or Goddesses had been on the island. And all that showed them was that they were as petty and vain as the stories made them out to be.

"Darrold is the pixie princess." Jana smiled at their

expressions. They looked back at Darrold who just grinned at them. She wasn't very tall, but she still was not as small as any pixie they had seen. Shaking their heads, they looked her over. Their thoughts were the same. Pixies were supposed to be young looking not grey-haired with wrinkles.

Darrold snorted at them as if she could read their thoughts. "Not like you all are cream of the crops for Guardians. You remind me of a bunch of mamby pambies."

"Mamby pambies?" Cole looked affronted at that description.

"Why doesn't she live in Sanctuary?" I.Q. asked, something that had them all curious. I.Q. wanted to distract Cole who looked as if he was about to argue with Darrold.

"Most of our mythicals don't live in our Sanctuary. This isn't the lower 48," Cameron told them. Their gazes all ventured to Gage who was watching Darrold, not looking at them. "Actually, very few live in our Sanctuary."

"Most live among the populace of Alaska, and those we check in on to make sure they are okay and that they don't need anything," Nat told them leaning on the rail of Darrold's deck.

"With most of the mythicals they barely tolerate our visits," Wes told them before giving Darrold one of those player smiles. "But Darrold likes us."

"So you think," Darrold told him, but they could all see the twinkle in her eye.

"I am a platinum member! Seat me now!" Nikos demanded distracting them.

"What is he going on about?" Cole looked at the bird whose colorful wings were spread wide in agitation as he squawked.

"Ignore him," Darrold told them. "He used to live in a hotel."

"What does that have to do with what he is talking about?" Chance looked confused, but Darrold just shrugged.

It was a laughing Wes who answered, "In hotels, they have some customers who pay to be platinum members, which is a nice way of allowing them to make outrageous demands that hotel workers have no choice but to make happen."

Chapter 5

"Dog sled racing! That is so cool."

Vanna glared at Chance whose eyes were lit up with excitement.

"Oh, come on Van, you even spoke with the dogs who said they were happy and treated well," Chad reminded her before she could make the seaweed that was floating in the aquarium walls all around them attack his brother. She just grumbled at that.

He was speaking the truth. After they had left Darrold's, Vanna had pointed out all the dogs they heard barking. There were many houses that had over a dozen kennels with dogs in them. When they were told that the dogs were bred for dog sled racing, Vanna had immediately protested and walked right up to the kennels to speak with the dogs. The dogs were happy with their lives and had told her how well they were treated, much to her irritation.

It also didn't help that Wes was an Iditarod racer. Vanna kept sending him dirty looks. Nothing anyone said to her would change her mind. They were just going to have to keep an eye on her and hope the town didn't end up overcome by Iditarod dogs.

Lights started flashing all around them, and sirens echoed down the hallways.

"Shadows?"

Telara came to a stop; that was the same type of alarms that were sounded back home at their Sanctuary. She looked at Cameron and Lyla who nodded at them before racing down the hallway to their command room with the Guardians following.

As they entered the command room, the view outside the glass had them stopping in awe. The coral palace was lit up so that the water all around them was bright with many colors. They were told the palace was several miles from the Command Center; yet, looking out the command room's glass walls, it looked as if it was much closer. They could see fishes of all types, sizes, and colors swimming around right outside. They could see mermen and mermaids all in armor and military formations patrolling the outskirts of their kingdom.

"The merpeople are readying their defenses, prepared to attack if the Shadows come this way. Protocol for any Shadow attack is that all mythicals are ready for an attack on their home front."

They turned and saw Kayne standing there, his hair still very unkempt, but his eyes staring out at the water with an extremely focused stare. His words were tight.

"Where are the Shadows?" Telara asked him, looking out the glass as if expecting to see them fighting with the mermaids.

"Wasilla," Shayne told them, and Kayne's expression went from just being focused to one of almost horror. Shayne gave a tight nod. "Darrold."

They turned to see Lyla along with her Faction gearing up with Crims: illusion crystals along with some healing crystals. Seeing the healing crystals, they frowned.

"I thought only healers were able to use the healing crystals?" Vanna said all their thoughts.

Lyla shrugged as she pulled her hair back into a ponytail. "Here in Alaska we all need to know how to heal ourselves. Alaska is a wild land, and you are taught from a young age how to take care of yourself."

"We wanna go with you." Tia stepped forward.

Lyla didn't say anything just nodded. "We could use the help; we will be using porters this time. Much faster."

They nodded and followed them to a room they recognized as a porter room. They were handed glasses and instantly put them on. This time, Zeke joined them as well as Gage, all geared up even though Gage couldn't use his Crim. Nothing more was said as the room around them glowed brightly taking them to their destination.

When the light faded, they were once again standing in front of Darrold's home. This time, instead of being surrounded by homemade lawn ornaments, there were Shadows all over. Not just the troll-like Shadows they fought last year either. Not even the ones that were like giants. These were very different; some were almost human-like while others resembled the wildlife that lives in the wilds of Alaska.

"Well, what are you guys standing there for?"

They turned around to see Darrold standing on her porch glaring at them from beneath her white bushy brows.

"Get rid of these things."

One of the creatures got close to her. Instead of panicking, she grabbed a crystal off of her porch railing and threw it at the Shadow. The Shadow screamed out in pain as the crystal exploded in a bright light.

"Do I have to do all the work myself?"

Chance just stared at her before Vanna shouted at him.

"Look out!"

He turned in time, pulling out his Crim and, with one whack of the flail, sent the more humanoid creature screaming away from him.

"She is a crazy old lady," Cole's face lit with mirth as he joined the fray with his nunchucks twirling in a blaze of fire and light. "I like her."

Telara just shook her head moving with the others to surround and protect Darrold from the human-like Shadows that were attempting to kidnap the pixie princess. I.Q. pulled back his bow letting his electric arrows fly, knocking back two Shadows.

"Squawk! I am a platinum member! Get these intruders out of my room! Rose petals in my bath!" Nikos was flapping around them squawking up a storm, especially when a Shadow attempted to grab him by his tail feathers which caused the very indignant bird to squawk, "I am a platinum member! What are you going to do about it?"

"Dammit, Nikos! Get out of here!" Wes glared at the bird lifting his own cross bow and letting a volley of arrows fly at once. He managed to hit the Shadow that was reattempting to capture the bird and knocked it back, along with several others that had gotten too close to the porch.

Wow. He can shoot more than one arrow at once.

They felt the same amazement as Chad. Then, looking at I.Q., they looked away; he looked a bit envious.

Don't worry, bud. I'm sure you'll master it soon

enough, Cole said quickly, but they could feel the damage was already done.

I.Q. wouldn't stop until he was able to shoot more than one arrow at a time. Telara was sure there would be many scorch marks in the training room when they got home. I.Q. wasn't a very vain person, but he also couldn't accept that anyone could do something better than him. The only thing that had kept him in line during their first visit to Sanctuary was the fact that it was all new, they were all learning. Now, I.Q. needed to accept they were still learning, not easy for someone as smart as I.Q. who was used to being the top student in everything.

"Don't forget that these Shadows could be innocents," Vanna hollered using her staff to knock a Shadow's legs out from under it. As it landed on the ground, she placed her staff on its chest. They watched as it glowed, and the glow engulfed the Shadow. They heard the screams but when the glow subsided, there on the ground lay...the Shadow.

They stood there in shock along with Zeke and Gage; the latter was fighting off the Shadows with crystal bombs and a crystal baton that was made just for him. Even though he couldn't control a Crim, Claw had made sure he didn't come unarmed. The Alaskans, however, looked confused.

"That was anti-climactic." Kaleb, a member of the Alpha Faction, looked at them quizzically. His freckled face showed his confusion beneath his bright red hair as he stood there looking down from his height of 6 feet.

"He should've reverted to his normal self." Vanna was staring down at her staff and the Shadow creature that was still unconscious at her feet.

A very low, melodious, sinister laughter filled the air

around them. When they turned, they saw a cloaked figure standing on the wrought iron archway over one of the many paths in Darrold's garden. The hand that they could see peeking out of her dark robes was so pale it was almost opaque; the nails were long and pointed as well as painted black. She pointed to Vanna, her voice carrying down to them.

"You are the one who has been undoing all my hard work with the Shadows," her voice accused Vanna.

"Yes!" Vanna hollered back, her eyes bright with emotion. "And I will keep undoing your handiwork until all the innocents are freed."

More laughter as the cloaked figure watched them. "I do not think so little Guardian. You have been finding it harder and harder to rid the Shadows of their darkness, have you not?"

Telara felt a shiver run down her spine; there was something familiar about this person. The person from her dream-walk with Zach; a Shadowmaker, wasn't she? No, wait! That was the creature that wheezed. Wasn't it? Too many things had happened in the past year; it was hard to keep them straight in her head. Her dream-walk with the mysterious Zach who always visited her in her dreams, except that one time after the big battle, seemed longer than a year ago at times.

"We will defeat you!" Gage's voice rang out around them. Telara could hear the fear and fury in his voice. He must be remembering that night as well. His memory would be more traumatic of course.

"The one that got away," the figure said softly and slowly to him, as if she was speaking to a child. "No worries. We will welcome you home soon enough."

"Like hell you will." He threw a crystal bomb at the figure dispersing the Shadows that were surrounding her like marbles across a floor although the figure remained standing there, staring at them from beneath the hooded cloak. Her laughter mocked Gage's attempt.

"I am not a Shadow to run from the light little boy; I am the light," she laughed. "From the light comes the Shadows. Enough of this." She turned to the Shadows that seemed to be waiting. "Get me the princess!"

Her words incited the Shadows that were being held back by the Crims and crystals. Now, they moved forward along with some other Shadows that appeared as if out of nowhere. They started fighting these Shadows, not wanting to do any serious harm but knowing they couldn't let them get their hands on Darrold.

The battle turned against them when a Shadow changed its form from a human to a bear, attacking two of the Alpha Faction team members. The bear form seemed to be able to take more pain from the Crims and crystals, enough that the bear was able to swipe its claws and injure the small redhead of the Alpha Faction.

"What the..."

"Hades?" Vanna finished for the very dumbfounded I.Q. Even the two Factions looked as surprised as they were. It seems this was something new to them as well, but they couldn't dwell on the matter; they needed to protect Darrold and fight against the Shadows.

"We're going to need more than just the crystals, Telly," Tia said, and everyone nodded in agreement as they looked around for something more to help them.

The plants in Darrold's little gardens started to grow, creating walls between them and the Shadows.

"Way to go, Van," Chance was cheering. The Alpha and Theta Factions looked impressed. It didn't last long as the Shadows seemed to faze through the shrubbery wall.

"That isn't good. I thought they were solid?" I.Q. stared, his mouth dry. "They could only disappear in Shadows."

They looked at Gage and the other Alaskan Factions that were watching the Shadows with a grim expression.

"Yeah, well, maybe you should tell them that," Cole said, his voice tight with tension.

The Shadows started towards them, some shifting into bears and even wolves. The winds picked up around them as Tia used the air to push back the Shadows. One Shadow grabbed onto one of the smaller girls in the Alpha group pulling her back with it.

"Lana!" Nat shouted.

Cole leapt forward, his blazing nunchucks twirling as he brought them down on the creature's wrist, causing it to let Lana go as it howled out in pain.

Telara used her Rotary to pull them both out of the way as a Shadow that had changed its shape to that of a python lunged for them. I.Q. and Wes both sent arrows at the python. I.Q. added an extra electrical charge to his that shocked the creature so much that it changed its shape to something more humanoid looking.

Maybe that is their original form? Tia wondered, but there wasn't any time for discussion. The other Shadows weren't stopping in their advance.

"I am a platinum member!" Nikos was flying around their heads, making himself more of a target for the Shadows as well as making it harder on the fighters.

They had to keep the Shadows from Darrold and him.

"Nikos! Stay still," Chance's voice growled in agitation as he used the water in a nearby bird bath to knock a Shadow from the bird.

"Focus!" Brandon barked at them.

"You try focusing with a crazy bird squawking about being a stupid platinum member! I'm about ready to take away his membership," Telara muttered as she formed a force shield of sorts and used it to push back Shadows that were getting too close. "This is getting ridiculous. Can't we just port her back to your Sanctuary?"

"Sure," Wes nodded at her. "If you want to chance bringing a few of these Shadows with us."

"Well, at least at Sanctuary we can contain them," Chad muttered.

Lyla knocked a Shadow down with her staff and glowered at him. "Considering we have never seen shapeshifting Shadows before, exactly how do you propose we do that?"

They didn't have an answer for that, but they were all getting tired. No matter how many Shadows they pushed back, knocked back, or blasted back with their rapidly diminishing supply of crystal bombs, more just took their place.

How long had they been fighting already? They looked into the sky and while the sun had gone down some, it was still bright out, so it couldn't be as long as it felt. A roar had them turning around, and the feeling of the ground shaking had them all just a bit nervous. From the woods came Shadows in the shapes of bears, moose, caribou, and wolves. It was a stampede, and they were right in the way.

"Scatter!" Lyla shouted, but they had already been jumping from the porch and landing hard on the ground, the stones from Darrold's driveway cutting into their arms, cheeks, and hands as they landed.

"My porch!" Darrold, standing behind Wes, could be heard screaming in dismay.

"This place is being overrun by Shadows, and she is worrying about her porch?" I.Q. looked over at Telara who just shrugged, turning around just as a Shadow appeared and grabbed her, tossing her into the little garden flats in Darrold's yard. She groaned as her head hit one of the iron bedrails.

"My celery! Get out of my garden!" Darrold shouted at her.

She moaned as she was helped by Chance out of the celery bed. Looking up into the still lit sky, she tried to shout a warning, but it was too late. A Shadow in the shape of a big bird swooped down and grabbed Darrold in one clawed foot. It shot upwards as Wes and I.Q. both shot arrows after it.

"Don't hit Darrold dang it!" Lyla smacked Wes hard, although it didn't look like it even fazed him; he just frowned down at her. "If you harm her, the King and Queen will have our heads on a platter."

Wes gestured to the sky. "And that is better?"

"At least she is alive! Now, we just need to find her," Lyla said aggravated and looking around them. The Shadows all around them suddenly disappeared; it seemed that they had what they had come for. All that was left was the yard that was in shambles. She looked at Cameron.

"Send Jesse when you get back; we'll do our best to

track them until he meets up with us." She reached up, grabbed Wes by his collar, and dragged him after her.

⊗)[)⊗

Gage had them looking around for evidence of any remaining Shadows, but nothing could be found. They were completely gone.

"Well, I guess we better tell Shayne to get you guys rooms," Nat said, and Brandon smirked. They weren't sure why.

That was, until Cameron chuckled. "She'll like that; all the nymphs will be down for the night which means she'll have to get the rooms ready."

"And heaven forbid Fifth Avenue actually do menial work," Lana, the one Cole had saved earlier, said with a flip of her hair.

"Your nymphs go to bed early here," Cole snickered.

"Early?" Cameron frowned at them.

"Cole, it is two in the morning," Gage spoke up, and Cole wasn't the only who was frowning.

"Yeah, dude. Here in Alaska during the summertime the sun doesn't ever set. It just goes down until it looks like dusk then rises again," Zeke told him.

"Really?" Chad was grinning, and Telara was sure whatever he was thinking, she didn't want to know. He had some of the strangest thoughts at times. He and Cole. "So, I bet your vampires aren't very happy with that."

One of the other Alpha members just shrugged. He was a tall, lanky, red head with freckles dotting his cheeks and nose. Telara was sure they had said Kaleb was his name. "They get a lot of rest in the summertime but watch out in the wintertime. Only a few hours of sleep a day makes for cranky vamps."

"Wait!" Cole stopped and looked at him. "Are you serious? There are really vampires here?"

Telara and Tia looked at each other, not wanting to admit they were wondering the same thing. The Alpha Faction didn't answer him; he just told them to get their shades ready for porting back to Sanctuary.

"Oh, come on." Chad was still complaining as the world around them lit up, signifying that they were being ported back to Sanctuary.

Chapter 6

The rooms they were given were nothing like their rooms back in Sanctuary unless you were talking about Chance's. The walls around them were glass, so they could see the sea life swimming around along with the mermaid warriors who were patrolling the sound floor; after Darrold had been taken, they were told that all of the mythical tribes were being vigilant. This beat the view of Mermaid Lake that Chance had back home in his room.

Telara sat down on her bed realizing how exhausted she was. The sky might be bright above the water, but it was still very late. Laying back, she closed her eyes to let sleep welcome her in its slumbering embrace.

"Miss me?"

A smile curved her lips as she rose up from her prone position to see Zach leaning against the glass wall surrounding her room.

"Hello, stranger." She had to admit she had missed him. Since the island, he hadn't been to visit her, and she had begun to think that he wouldn't again. "I didn't think I would see you again."

He tilted his head looking at her. "You thought I would leave you without telling you goodbye?"

She shrugged because she honestly didn't know him well enough to answer that question.

He walked over to her taking her hands in his. She looked up at him. "How about if I make a promise that if I were to ever leave and not return, I will make sure to say goodbye first?"

"Don't make promises you can't keep."

A dimple appeared on his left cheek that she had never noticed before. "I never do."

With a slight incline of her head she agreed. "Okay then."

Zach looked out through the walls where they could see a couple of bright orange fish play a game of tag. "Nice place they have up here."

"Never been here?" She frowned as she realized she really didn't know anything about him. She knew he was a past Guardian, but nothing beyond that; he spoke in worse riddles than Lucius. Although, to be fair, Lucius didn't completely speak in riddles; he just didn't tell them everything.

A small shake of his head answered her question.

"So, you don't know what's going on then?" she asked, her voice full of disappointment. She had hoped he was here to give her some advice.

His shoulders lifted in a shrug. "Never said that."

"So?"

"How much do you know about the legends and myths of Alaska?"

She truly didn't know how to answer that. "What does that have to do with the Shadow attack today?"

He raised a brow at her, giving her a begrudging shrug.

She responded to his question. "Nothing."

"Alaska is a very magical place, and nothing is more

magical than their legends and myths," Zach told her watching a mermaid warrior with great interest as he spoke. "Their legends and myths are so important to them that each legend or myth is protected by a different mythical tribe."

"I still don't know what that has to do with them taking Darrold."

"She was a pixie princess, correct?"

"Yes."

"Each tribe is tasked with a legend, and one person of the tribe is the protector of said legend. To find out why she was taken, you need to discover her job, if she had one, as well as the legend with which her tribe was entrusted."

"So, you're saying the Shadows had another reason for taking Darrold other than just her magical essence?"

Telara was starting to get a bad feeling about this. She had always thought of the Shadows as mindless creatures that were just attracted to magical essence. Zach's words meant that the Shadows are able to think and plan. If that is the case, then they were in serious trouble.

"Darrold was a protector of a legend here in Alaska?"

Zach shrugged. "That is a question for the King and Queen."

"What if she wasn't a protector of a legend?"

"Then you have a mystery on your hands."

She snorted at that; that seemed to be a daily occurrence for them anymore. Her mind swirled around all that she had learned here in Alaska, on the cursed island, and at Sanctuary itself, not to mention the Shadows that were able to change shape. Speaking of which... She looked up, but Zach was gone. She groaned and fell back on her bed. Figures.

They followed Gage, Zeke, and Cameron through Sanctuary tunnels under the water. These were glass tunnels under the water along the sound floor, so far under the water it was dark as night although they could see clearly all around them. Cameron pointed out the crystals along the glass tunnels that lit everything up.

They got to see Briny swimming by, blowing kisses towards Chance whose face was tinged pink. There were many other mermaids that were swimming around; most of them were the warriors in their armor. They even saw the one who thought he was king; he was picking up shells from the floor and putting them on his head. Of course, there were some noticeably big, ugly looking fish with bulging eyes that kept stealing the shells from his head.

Chad and Cole were getting a kick out of watching the poor merman yelling and throwing shells at the fish, to no avail.

The tunnel opened to another room that was larger than their cafeteria back in their Sanctuary. It looked even larger than the sports arena back home that had two football fields, a baseball diamond, and batting cages in it. There were tables of different sizes and shapes all over. At the head of the room were serving tables with foods of all kinds just like back home.

Eggs, bacon, pancakes, toast; you name it, it was there. They loaded their plates and grabbed a seat chatting with Gage, Zeke, Cameron, Brandon, and the other Alphas along with a few others they hadn't met. One was introduced as Paul, Shayne's second and, according to Brandon, the only one that could truly handle Shayne.

"Have you heard from Wes?" Brandon was shoveling the eggs into his mouth.

Paul shook his head. "Jesse and the Deltas joined them shortly after we got back. Still haven't heard from the Thetas yet."

"Jesse won't return until he has his mark," Zeke said as he reached for a piece of toast. "If he does, that won't be a good sign."

Their mark...Darrold. Telara looked down at her eggs and bacon and felt her stomach do somersaults. It was almost like Déjà vu; the flashbacks to when they lost Gage were still fresh.

"Why is that?" Chad asked.

"Because that means there is nothing to find," Paul spoke up looking down at his phone.

"Missing your bestie already?"

They looked up to see Shayne's mocking smile being directed at Paul as she spoke in her soft, serene voice. While her voice sounded as if she was mocking him, her hand on his shoulder said something different as well as the way she was looking at him.

Paul didn't even look up at her as he responded. "Don't you have some filing to do? Or, better yet, sit down and eat some actual food instead of that rabbit food you eat."

Shayne stiffened at his words before walking away. They looked at Paul, but he was already chatting with Gage between mouthfuls of eggs and bacon.

Am I wrong or was Shayne flirting with him? Tia said mentally trying to not look like she had been watching.

And he pretty much snubbed her. Cole was watching

Shayne walk away with an amused look, not even attempting to hide the fact that he was watching. Tia elbowed him hard enough to have him choking on his food.

Next time no mind speaking with your mouth full.

Chance snickered looking down at his plate while the others looked at them. Gage gave them weird looks; Telara was sure he figured it had something to do with their mind speak. She just grinned at him.

"You have a message from Pam," Gage told her between bites of breakfast.

"Is everything okay?"

This was the first mission they had gone on without Pam since they had become Guardians. She felt a bit guilty as she hadn't even thought about their friend since coming here.

"She said to make sure you guys were getting some training in while sightseeing," Gage told them, his lips twitching.

Telara couldn't stop the grin that spread across her face while Cole and Chad groaned. That was their friend! Pam was fun to hang around with, but she was still and always would be the Alpha leader.

"You can tell her not to worry."

"Good! She says she will see what new techniques you have learned when we get back."

Hearing that, the groans of the Guardians filled the room.

After breakfast, they had been summoned to one of the great rooms in Sanctuary to meet with the pixie King and Queen. They were informed to be very mindful of their words with the King and Queen. They were royalty after all and held seats on the mythical ruling council. This council decides all the decisions of the mythical tribes in Alaska as well as the Sanctuary itself. It would seem that the leaders of Sanctuary didn't have any influence over the mythicals, at least not here. They sat around a large oval table in the center of the room with at least thirty chairs around it. There were counters along a wall with beverages and snacks lined up for everyone as well.

They were sitting there with Kayne, Gage, Zeke, the Alpha team, the Theta team (who had returned without any luck), and the King and Queen of the pixies. The King stood in human form, tall and regal. His Queen stood next to him with her platinum blond hair pulled back under her sparkly crown. The crown was made up of silver twigs entwined and embellished with silver crystals. While the dark-haired King stood in silver robes over a bluish shirt and pants, the Queen practically glowed in her silver and blue flowing dress.

"Aren't pixies supposed to be tiny little things with wings?"

Telara wanted to sew Chad's lips together as he stared at the King and Queen as if waiting for them to answer his most idiotic question.

"Ouch!"

She sent a silent thanks to whoever hit him. She gave the King and Queen a very apologetic smile. "You will have to excuse our friend; he tends to speak before he thinks."

The King raised one aristocratic brow as he looked her way making her squirm under his gaze. She silently berated Chad who was grumbling that he thought it was a valid question. The king turned to address Chad.

"We can be our original size, which is the size of a doll and our most preferred form, or we can be the size of a human. With the danger to our daughter, we chose to meet with Sanctuary where we could look each of you in the eyes." His words were spoken clearly. Being a king, he was used to speaking, of course; however, they could hear the emotion behind the words.

Chad nodded to him as the King introduced himself and his Queen to the Guardians whom he had never met before.

"I am Kaleth, and this is my wife Juneth. We are honored to meet the Guardians and wish it could be on better terms."

Kayne stood up and grasped Kaleth's hand, his look somber. Lyla stood up looking just as somber as Kayne. It was Lyla who addressed the King.

"I am sorry Your Majesties. We were unable to find where the Shadows have taken your daughter."

Juneth placed a hand over her mouth trying to hold back a frightened gasp. Everyone in the room felt the emotion of guilt and sadness that sat heavily in their guts.

"We will find your daughter, and we will bring her home," Vanna told the King and Queen.

"The Theta Faction are our best trackers, and they were unable to find the princess. Nothing against the Guardians, but what makes you think you can do what they can't?" Kayne asked.

"The same way we learned how to heal the Shadows."

Kayne watched Vanna carefully as she spoke.

"It is teamwork that gets the job done, and it will be teamwork that will bring the princess home. We won't give up."

Gage, Zeke, and both the Alpha and Theta Factions all nodded in agreement. Telara tried to bite back the grin that threatened to spread at Vanna's words. When Vanna put her mind to something, she wouldn't give up until she had accomplished what she set out to do.

"We appreciate everything and if there is anything we can do to help, please let us know." Juneth's spoke in her gentle way.

"Actually, there is something." Everyone turned to look at Telara. "I don't suppose you could tell me what your job here in Alaska is?"

She could feel the confusion through the mental connection she had with her friends, she hadn't had time to explain to them about her dream with Zach. Kaleth and Juneth turned hard stares on her but she refused to take back the question.

"Would you care to explain what you mean by that question?" Kaleth's smooth regal voice held a hard edge now.

"Telara." Kayne's voice held a bit of warning in it, but she ignored it. Zach had never steered them wrong before.

"Which legend do you protect?"

The room went silent. The king looked at her with very sharp eyes. She had never understood that description before, but she sure did now.

"You are very well informed for an outsider."

Clipped words let Telara know that what Zach had told her was information that wasn't well-known.

"You could say that I'm in contact with a seer of sorts," Telara told him.

"And this seer informed you of something that is a

very well-kept secret? A secret that is so well guarded that many have lost their lives over it?"

She hadn't known that and, right now, she really wanted to strangle Zach for not telling her that part. The room went silent as the King stood there staring at her and waiting for her answer. Her lips were suddenly dry.

What is going on?

Chance's voice sound worried, but he looked ready to battle if needed.

That wasn't supposed to happen; she was just trying to figure out what was going on and now she was worried she might have caused some trouble they might not be able to get out of.

Zach came to me in my dream last night.

Why didn't you tell us that before you pissed off the kingly dude? Cole's face was straight as he watched Kaleth, but his tone in their mind link was anything but calm.

I didn't have time. Telara's was just as tense.

Ummmm, guys. He is waiting for an answer. I.Q. nudged them mentally, and Telara realized the whole room was staring at them, except for Gage and Zeke who were used to their mind speaking.

"It would seem so," she admitted. "I'm not here to cause problems or try to scream your secrets to the world. We just want to help. I was told that knowing the legend you protected would help us find Darrold and defeat the Shadows, which is something we all want."

Chapter 7

"What does The Sleeping Lady have to do with the Shadows and why they took my little girl?" Juneth asked, ignoring the frown from her husband.

"The Sleeping Lady?" Tia sounded as confused as Telara felt.

Kaleth opened his mouth to protest, but Juneth put up her hand stopping him. "If it helps us get our daughter home then I will tell them everything. They already know some of our duty; we might as well tell them the rest." She raised a delicate shoulder, the sparkly blue gown moving with her.

Her husband frowned then gave a sigh of defeat and nodded. "If everyone will please take a seat, we will tell you all that we can." Juneth took a seat giving her husband an encouraging smile.

Kayne glanced over at Telara for just a moment with a thoughtful look before moving back to his seat and giving Kaleth and his wife his full attention.

"Our legends are important to the people of Alaska. They are protected by the magical tribes. Each tribe has its own legend that it is tasked with protecting. Each tribe assigns one of its own to be the protector. We pixies were tasked with The Sleeping Lady."

"What is The Sleeping Lady?" Cole asked when it seemed that they were the only ones who were curious.

Considering they had never been to Alaska, how were they expected to know?

"The Sleeping Lady is the one legend of Alaska that is probably the most shared." As the King spoke, the air above the table shimmered and an image of a mountain appeared. "What I am about to tell you, you can find in any bookstore in Alaska. This story is told in books and also by word of mouth."

Kaleb stood up and showed them how the mountain resembled the form of a sleeping lady on her side.

The King spoke, his deep voice echoing in the quiet of the room. "Long ago, there lived a tribe of Gentle Giant people. The Giant people loved their land where they lived in peace and harmony. The children played and danced while the adults talked of their land that stretched into the inlet by the sea."

As he spoke, the image of the mountain changed to show a visual of the story he was telling. They could see children playing while adults were telling their stories.

"In this tribe was a couple who were named Susitna and Nekatla. These two loved each other so much that even their people loved their devotion to each other."

Now, the image was of a young couple who did indeed look very much in love.

"One day, a stranger visited the Giant People. He told them stories of a fierce and warlike tribe that lived far to the north. The stranger warned that they would one day be attacked by the warlike tribe."

They listened to his voice, but their eyes were on the changing images above the table. The images matched the King's words.

"The Great Chief of the Giant People gathered the

tribe together in council. The Giant People decided that all of the men, young and old, would travel north to convince the warlike tribe to live in peace and harmony."

"Susitna and Nekatla knew they would be separated for a long time. They walked hand in hand to their favorite plateau, overlooking the slender inlet. Nekatla gazed into Susitna's tearful eyes and promised her that he would return. He asked that she wait at this spot, as he wanted to find her as soon as he returned."

"Many days and nights passed with no sign of the Giant men or Nekatla. Susitna wove baskets and picked berries, but she grew weary and lay down on the plateau and was soon fast asleep. Meanwhile, the Giant People's men arrived at the northern Warlike Village."

"Their plea for peace and harmony was met with a swift and terrible answer. Suddenly, the Warlike Tribe attacked the Giant People. The battle was fierce but short. Many of the Giant People were killed, and others were taken prisoner."

Vanna gasped at the images while Telara felt her stomach clench and had to look away when one of the Giant People was attacked in a very bloodthirsty manner.

"The news of the disaster quickly swept across the Great Land. The name Nekatla was on everyone's lips for he, too, had fallen. With his last breath, he spoke the name of his precious Susitna. The women of the Giant People couldn't bear to awaken Susitna and tell her the fateful news. To shield her from heartbreak, they wove a blanket of grass and wildflowers then gently placed it over her sleeping form."

"That night, the women prayed to their Gods to place Susitna in a deep, unawakening sleep. The Gods answered the women's prayers, but the price was high as the Great Land would be changed forever. The air turned cold, and a light snow began to cover Susitna and the long stretch of land that ran into the inlet. That snow was the first that had fallen in the Great Land."

Telara felt her eyes tearing up at the vision; she felt so sorry for Susitna. At the same time, she realized that these were Giants. Giants were just as magical as other mythical creatures.

"Days turned into years, and Susitna continued to sleep and dream of Nekatla's return. The Giant People disappeared from the Great Land, and different smaller people came in their place to watch over the sleeping Susitna. Each summer, her sleeping body is still covered by the blanket of grass and wildflowers, and each winter the Gods gently place a soft blanket of snow upon her."

"Some say that when all the warring people of the world disappear, when peace and harmony return to this world, that Nekatla will awaken his sleeping Susitna. The mountain is called Mount Susitna but to those of us that know the truth, we call her the Sleeping Lady."

The image went back to the mountain in the form of a sleeping lady. Telara's hands were cold.

"Now, I will tell you what you won't find in any book."

Telara wasn't sure she wanted to know, not considering what was already going through her mind with what she saw on the screen.

"Our people were entrusted with this legend; we alone have the ability to wake The Sleeping Lady from her slumber."

Telara looked over at her friends whose faces wore

the same worried expression as they realized exactly what this would mean. Their faces were white with worry.

"But only in the event of Nekatla's return," The King told them. "My daughter holds the key to awakening Susitna, as it is the youngest of the royal family that holds that responsibility."

"Darrold is the youngest?" Chad's eyes were wide. "But she was an old lady - ouch!" He glared at I.Q. who looked pointedly at the King and Queen who didn't look amused. "Sorry," he mumbled.

Would be nice if he would think before he speaks.

Telara nodded in agreement to Tia but was also thankful Chad was too busy rubbing his sore shin to hear.

The King looked at Chad, and his words were spoken tightly. "I am 600 years old, my wife a mere 450 years old, and our youngest is 121 years old. We choose our appearance as Darrold chooses hers."

"Your Highness," Gage spoke up respectfully, and Kaleth nodded to him. "Is it possible for Darrold to waken Susitna without Nekatla returning?"

Kaleth frowned. "Why would my daughter do such a thing?"

"She might not want to, but the Shadowmaster and his minions might try to force her," Telara answered trying to make her words as soft as possible, knowing there was no easy way to put it.

"My daughter would never do such a thing!" Kaleth's chest puffed out, and his face grew red with indignation.

"Your highness," Kayne spoke up keeping his tone very respectful and calm. "We mean no disrespect."

Kaleth gave him a look of disbelief. "You know the power of the Shadows and what we have been fighting; we need to look at all angles."

Kaleth went from an indignant king to suddenly a very weary one as he sat down in the chair next to his wife. He looked almost beaten, more like a worried father than a pompous king.

"My daughter is in the hands of those creatures." He looked up at Kayne, and his eyes showed his worry. "I just want her safe back in her little home."

"I understand, your highness. I promise you that Sanctuary and the Guardians will do their best to make that happen." Everyone nodded in agreement.

"Excuse me, your highness?"

Kaleth looked at I.Q. who had raised his hand as if they were in school. He gave a nod.

"Is there by any chance a failsafe if Susitna were to be awoken prematurely?"

"Failsafe?" The King frowned at his words.

"You know, a backup plan if your daughter was forced to awaken the giantess," Gage said drawing the King's attention. He gave Gage an affronted look.

"Of course, we do!"

There was a sigh of relief around the room. "That's good." Telara smiled at the King finally feeling as if maybe they could get through this. "So, what is it?"

The King gave a sheepish look which, considering all the strong emotions he had shown since entering the room, looked very out of place. "Darrold took care of that."

Everyone groaned.

"I am sure whatever plan my daughter put in place

will be shown when it is needed; there is no need to worry."

Gage stared at the man, but it was Layla who stood up and addressed the king.

"No disrespect to you, your wife, your daughter, or even your people, but we can't just sit and trust in your daughter blindly when our home is in such danger. If Susitna wakes without her love there, the chaos that will be brought to our world could destroy all that we have protected and created."

"And if the Shadows control her, that is going to be a hundred times worse," Chance interjected.

Kaleth glared at Telara as if this was all her fault. "Better to trust in my daughter than silly dreams."

"We are going to take everything into consideration, your highness," Kayne spoke up, which was probably a good thing considering Telara had opened her mouth to speak.

"The fate of my daughter is in your hands; Kayne and you will be the one held accountable if anything happens to her," he said looking directly at Telara.

Kayne nodded. "Of course."

"You should get the moose but make sure to tell them you want it half and half," a dark-skinned girl walking by their table spoke up when Cole said he wasn't sure what he wanted. Her dark braids swayed with her movements.

Telara looked around the room they were in. It was a local tavern that was run by a relative of Silest's Cameron told them. They had yet to meet this relative, but the waitstaff were forest nymphs. Gnomes could be seen clearing tables. The hand behind the food counter that hit the bell stating an order was done looked to be larger than average. The flutter of wings could be heard all around them; Lyla said that was the sprites who were keeping the lanterns lit.

The tavern was located on one of the many islands in the Sound, hidden from mortal eyes by magic. The islands housed over 70% of the supernaturals that lived in Alaska they were told. Very few mortals ventured on the islands. And the scarce few that did venture on the island were kept from the villages with all the creatures living there by a magic barrier.

"Guardians, meet Nessie," Cameron told them dryly, and they could tell by his tone that they didn't get along. The way Nessie's eyes narrowed at him confirmed her sentiment. "She is an Omega under Beth."

Nessie did a pirouette on the ball of her foot and walked away; her head held high. Seven sets of curious eyes turned to look at him. Gage and Zeke just leaned back in their seats to watch the show with amused expressions.

"Nessie is the resident know-it-all," Cameron told them wryly. "She believes she is better than everyone else."

"No one can do anything right according to her," Lyla agreed her voice showing her irritation. "Only she knows how to do things right."

"From tying your shoes to breathing," Wes spoke up as he grabbed a chair and turned it around so he could straddle it. "Go over not under, breath out first then in," he mimicked Nessie causing the others to laugh.

"So, who is your pick for the Iditarod this year?" they heard a dark-haired gnome say as he lumbered over to a table close to theirs where his buddies all sat with their tankards already full.

"Definitely not that Cheechako from the lower 48," his companion muttered, his mouth inches from his tankard, and his brow furrowed into a frown. He sounded irritated, but none of them could understand why. Well, the Guardians couldn't understand why.

"What is a Cheechako?" Telara asked Jana, who was sitting next to her, very softly so as not to alert the gnome and his buddies that she had been eavesdropping. But it seemed from the quirk of Jana's lips that she knew why Telara had asked that question.

"Cheechako means someone new to living in Alaska, who is still wet behind the ears, and who has a lot to learn about Alaska," she explained. "The one they are talking about is some new guy from the lower 48, which is basically the other states," she explained when Telara looked perplexed. "He moved to Alaska a few years back and bought a whole Iditarod team that was already trained to race."

"What is wrong with that?" Telara was confused because Jana seemed to think that it was something funny.

"If you want to win the Iditarod, you train the team yourself. If you can't take the time to do that, then you might as well go surfing in a volcano," Paul said as he joined them, fist bumping Wes as he took his seat next to his buddy.

The whole tavern lifted their glasses as if in support of Paul's words. Telara still didn't understand what it mattered but, then again, she was worse than a Cheechako:

she wasn't new to living in Alaska; she was a visitor who had been there only days.

Even so, Alaska seemed like the perfect place to her, at least to visit. They had only seen a little of Alaska, but it was enough to make her want to see more. The air felt so alive and free; she couldn't remember ever feeling so at peace with herself. She saw a dark-haired woman enter the tavern swathed in a multicolored fur coat. Either the woman was very much on the heavy side, or that fur coat was exceptionally large. The woman's dark gaze was intense as she scanned the tavern, as if she were there with a purpose.

Paul's laughter had her turning back to the table where their food was being served.

"Well, doesn't help that she is a native."

"Native? Who?" Telara had been so distracted with her thoughts and the dark-haired fur-coated woman she wasn't listening to the conversation going on at her own table.

"Nessie," Tia told her before popping a fry in her mouth.

"What's wrong with her being a native?" Telara started eating her food as well.

"Tell me you guys don't hold that against a person." Vanna glared at the table, the plants around her moving in agitation.

Cameron held up his hands. "Whoa, calm down Mother Nature. We don't hold it against anyone if they are a native, sourdough, or Cheechako. It is the natives who hold that against someone."

Wes gave a quick nod. "To a native, you could be born in Alaska and not considered a true native unless you can trace your whole ancestry back to this place."

Vanna frowned. "Well, that isn't right either."

Wes shrugged. "That's the way it is little sister; some natives are more accepting than others, but all have that belief."

"Yeah, well that one chief who called Claw a Cheechako has made it very clear that he refuses to have anything to do with anymore Cheechakos after the incident with Claw," Cameron said between bites of food.

"Incident?" Cole, Chad, and Chance leaned forward their faces full of interest and their mouths full of burger to which Vanna protested when she could see their food.

"Let's just say when Claw asked what Cheechako meant, he didn't appreciate the definition," Wes answered.

Lyla glared at Wes who looked very unapologetic.

"You said the definition was someone who is new to Alaska?" Telara said confused.

Lyla looked at Wes who swallowed his bite of burger and took a drink before answering. Everyone at the table made sure to swallow their food as well, so Telara was sure it was going to be a good answer. She wasn't disappointed.

"Yes, and that was what Lee had told him."

That wasn't so bad she thought until Wes continued.

"Then someone else told him the short version was stupid white male."

"Ewwwww!"

Chad hadn't followed everyone else's example and swallow his food; instead, he spit it out when he laughed, and Vanna jumped up before it hit her. The guys at the table laughed even harder while the females glared at Chad.

"So," Lyla spoke up still giving Chad a dirty look. "Needless to say, Claw's reaction to that is what got him banned from Alaska."

"What did he do?" Tia looked at her, but it was Paul who answered.

"Let's just say he ruined the Chief's favorite headdress."

The laughter that erupted from the others at the table confused them but before they could ask for more specifics, there was a commotion from the other side of the tavern.

Chapter 8

Woman, what is your problem?"

A shaggy-haired gnome was shouting at the dark-haired woman with the fur coat that Telara had noticed earlier.

"Uh oh, what did Bobby do to upset Nan this time?" Wes asked with a grin.

"He better run if he values his fingers."

Paul took a big bite of his burger.

Jana sighed. "He has been told not to put up his traps on Nan's territory a million times."

Paul shrugged, continuing to eat his burger as the shouting got louder from the gnome and Nan started throwing pieces of her fur coat at him. Telara frowned. Nan was actually grabbing pieces of her fur coat and throwing them at the gnome.

"Bobby knows how protective she is over her animals. He wants to risk his fingers and nose trying to trap animals; I say he deserves what he gets."

"Wait, the woman with the 'fur' coat is protective over the animals?" Cole emphasized the fur part of her coat, but Paul just laughed.

"Just watch! That isn't an ordinary fur coat, man."

That was when Telara realized exactly what Nan was doing. She wasn't throwing pieces of the fur coat. She was throwing little furry creatures at Bobby who were grabbing onto his fingers and nose with their teeth. Nan's fur coat was alive!

"My babies are going to bite off your fingers you short piece of trapper meat," Nan screamed across the room, her long slim finger pointing at Bobby, who was jumping around and trying to pull what looked like a gopher off his nose.

"You guys have gophers here?" Telara asked Lyla who laughed.

"That is an Alaskan marmot." She nodded at Nan. "Her coat is full of marmots, otters, foxes, and mink. In fact, any mammal that can be found on many of the islands are in her coat."

Lyla wasn't kidding. Nan kept throwing animal after animal at Bobby and yet her coat still looked rather full.

"Nan is a nature nymph and a very protective one at that," Cameron laughed. "Then again, all nymphs are very protective of their element."

"And can be very vindicative."

Brandon stood up looking around at everyone while trying to avoid the flying fur babies of Nan's that was being thrown.

"I'm going to cut your beard off, you big nosed bully."

The whole tavern went silent at Nan's words, and Bobby's eyes widened as if in shock over her words.

"What happened?" I.Q. whispered, not wanting to speak too loudly in the silence.

"Telling a gnome you are going to cut off their beard is the worst insult you could levy at them," Lyla said looking around nervously as other gnomes started rising from their seats, their hard gazes on Nan.

"Worse than calling a native a Cheechako," Brandon

said as he looked around the tavern, his expression and actions just as alert as Lyla and the others. "Basically, cutting off a gnome's beard is like cutting their throat."

"Y-y-you furry loving female! I can't believe you would actually threaten such a thing," Bobby sputtered, his face bright red and his voice very indignant, which was something considering he was still pulling off furry mammals who were still trying to bite and gnaw on him.

Wes rose from his seat, tossed his napkin onto his plate, and nudged Paul who had just managed to eat the last bite of his burger.

"Looks like dinner time is over. When Kara finds out Nan and Bobby are going at it…"

"What is going on in my tavern?" A shrill voice echoed all around them.

"That is our cue," Cameron said, and they followed his lead, heading out the nearest door along with many others who had the same idea.

"What time is it? Seems like we've been up a lot longer."

Cole looked around them at the still bright sky. Paul, Wes, and the rest of the Theta Faction had headed back down below to Sanctuary. The Theta Faction were heading down to see if Jesse had sent back any word on Darrold while Paul had gotten a message from Shayne that he was needed. Therefore, after a little bit of joshing between Wes and Paul over Shayne, they had all separated.

The Guardians had stayed and were walking with the Alpha group around the island. Cameron looked at his watch answering Cole with a shrug.

"It's about two in the morning."

Cole gave a shake of his head. "That would be so hard to get used to." The others laughed at that.

"You don't like our midnight sun?" Nat chuckled, but Cole just frowned, so she explained. "That's what we call it between May and September when the sun doesn't really set."

"So, will we be able to see the northern lights while we are here?" Vanna asked with a hopeful expression.

"Sorry." Cameron gave an apologetic smile. "You came at the wrong time; it needs to be a bit darker here than it gets this time of summer."

Vanna looked so crestfallen that Brandon threw his arm around her shoulders, giving her a squeeze. "Just come back in a few months, and I'll show you the lights."

Ohhhhh man, Gabe would have a fit if he were here.

Vanna's face turned red, and she glared at Cole who was grinning from ear to ear, but Brandon was oblivious to the silent exchange. They really needed to watch it with their private chats, Telara thought. While Brandon was oblivious, Gage had caught the undercurrent and was frowning. Telara just shrugged her shoulders.

They had been walking in silence for a few minutes when Chance spoke out loud what was all on their minds.

"So, do we think the Shadows will be able to make Darrold awaken the Giantess?"

Cameron shrugged. "Most of the Shadows we ever fought were mindless creatures. Never once have we battled the Shadowmaster or has anyone actually seen him."

Gage looked down, and Telara remembered the dream walk that Zach had taken her on when Gage had been captured.

"The only other Shadows we have seen besides the minions and generals was a Shadowmaker and some female who looked nothing like a Shadow," Telara said so Gage didn't have to.

The whole Alpha group stopped and stared at her, but it was Cameron who spoke.

"Who is this Shadowmaker and female?"

Telara gave a shrug. "It was during a dream walk with Zach. That was when we found out the Shadows were actually friends and other magical creatures, not just Shadows. The woman we saw at Darrold's during the battle, she was also there with the person they called The Shadowmaker."

"Yeah, that news had many upset at our Sanctuary," Lana said not really looking at them.

"What? Why?" Telara was confused; she thought that would be good news all around.

Kaleb tried to reassure her with a friendly smile. "You have to understand that we have fought the Shadows for many years; we lost many friends to them and when you discovered that, it was a shock to us all."

"But why would it upset you to find out that your friends and family weren't completely lost?" Tia frowned at him.

"Because that meant we were fighting our friends and family," Nat said.

"Are you saying you would've rather not known?" I.Q. looked at her, his brow furrowing into a frown.

"Oh no, not at all," Lana was quick to correct. "But you have to realize we all lost friends and family to the Shadows."

"But now you know that you didn't really lose

them," Tia said, starting to realize what they meant but still wanting to reassure them.

Lana nodded. "And we don't even know if they are able to be saved or where they are."

"One day, all the Shadows will be gone, and everyone will be freed," Gage said. Telara smiled at Gage and nodded. She understood Lana's words and feelings, but if they only concentrated on the what ifs they would miss out on so much more.

"Yes, they will."

They walked in silence as they continued down the path. Knowing how late it was, Telara knew they needed to head back to Sanctuary. They needed some sleep. The air was quiet around them; it seemed the creatures were already sleeping. The sound of music was faint but could be heard on the wind.

"Is that music I hear?" Tia looked around.

Cameron chuckled. "That would be our resident musical recluse."

"Soliel?"

Everyone turned and looked at Telara in surprise.

"What?" She frowned.

"You know of Soliel?" Brandon stared at her.

She gave a shrug. "I met her when we were exploring one of the islands our first day here, but it wasn't this island." She looked at her friends. "She is Serdita's sister, the one they told us about back in Tellus." They gasped as they remembered being told about Soliel and the Chenras.

"She doesn't stick to just one island," Cameron said slowly watching her. "And she usually doesn't show herself to anyone either."

"Great, another magical being only Telara sees or talks to," Chad grumbled. "Ouch." He rubbed his arm where Vanna had hit him. He looked at Telara and muttered an apology.

She wanted to tell them how she hated it more than they did. She didn't ask for the creatures to come to her, to speak in riddles and make her feel as if she was losing her mind.

"What do you know of her?" Telara asked Cameron refusing to even acknowledge Chad's apology; she didn't care if it was petty of her or not. She was tired of them thinking she was getting special treatment when all she wanted was to live a normal life.

"The residents around here call her a cross between a prophet and a seer."

"I actually prefer the term Diviner, thank you."

Everyone turned around, and there she stood, violin in hand with her multi-colored hair flowing around her round face.

Telara grinned. Her own friends were staring at Soliel with something akin to a combination of curiosity and amazement, but their Alaskan friends looked as if they were frozen in time. They were staring at Soliel with wide eyes and mouths partially open. Telara turned to look at Soliel.

"Hello, Soliel. Good to see you again."

Soliel raised an eyebrow as if in disbelief, to which Telara couldn't help but laugh. Her friends were going from surprised to interested, but the Alaskans took just a bit longer to come out of their shocked stupor. Which, considering that they lived in a world of mythicals where they fought Shadows with crystals that turned into magical weapons, was something that was odd to Telara.

"We were just being told that you don't show yourself to many, in fact that I was the first non-mythical to see you."

Not very tactful but at this point Telara wasn't feeling very tactful. So many times, she felt as if she were in over her head, and she was tired of training just so her and the others could go to their deaths. At least if they had to do that, she was wanting answers and not more riddles.

Soliel just shrugged, lifted her violin/Chenra to her shoulder, and started playing. "Actually, I am just very choosy about who I speak to."

The air around them filled with the silver music notes that floated all around.

"So, why have you shown yourself now?"

Telara watched her move around, dancing to the music that was weaving all around her. She didn't want to take her eyes off of her; the last time she had done that, Soliel had disappeared.

"I was under the impression that you had some questions for me; if I am wrong, I can leave."

"NO!" Telara almost shouted. "Please don't leave. I do have some questions." She really hadn't been thinking of Soliel but since she was there in front of them, it wouldn't hurt to see if she could help them.

Soliel kept doing her dancing and playing the silver violin but said nothing, so Telara spoke up. "The last time we spoke, you said we were being lied to."

"That isn't a question," Soliel's lofty voice spoke over the melody in the air as she twirled around letting her head fall back and her multi-colored hair flow with her. "That is a statement."

"Okay, fine. What did you mean by that?"

"I don't believe I stuttered when I spoke. I always speak so very clearly. How could you not understand what I said?" A twirl here, a dip there, and with a leap Soliel landed on a small hill on the other side of them. Not once during the dance did she pause in her playing.

Telara breathed in deeply. This is what the others were jealous of? Being totally aggravated?

Sorry.

She jerked up; she hadn't realized that she had projected her thoughts. Her friends were looking very abashed and apologetic at her.

It's all right. I just really wish someone would actually be upfront with us for once. Come out and say what they mean.

Remember what Pam said?

Telara looked at Tia who spoke.

Seers, prophets, or even Diviners all speak in riddles. They cause more questions than they answer.

Don't remember her saying anything about Diviners. What is a diviner anyways? Cole spoke up, and Tia glared at him.

Guys! I.Q. gave very pointed looks at Gage, Zeke, and the others that were staring at them. Gage was used to their mind speak, but the others weren't. That didn't mean that it didn't irritate him and by the frown on his face they were pretty sure it was irritating him right now.

"Sorry." Telara grinned and turned to Soliel who hadn't paused in her playing nor her dancing during their exchange. "You said we were being lied to. Well, who is lying to us?"

"Actually, the question is who isn't," Soliel said as she

danced along the trail, keeping her distance from them.

"No, that isn't confusing." Telara's voice was dripping with aggravation.

"What are we being lied to about?" I.Q. asked keeping his eyes on Soliel as she danced all around them.

"Who you truly are."

Chapter 9

The Guardians looked at each other, each of them looking confused and even a bit apprehensive. It had been a year since discovering they were Guardians and yet they still felt as if they were floundering in quicksand at times. Like now.

"Who we truly are?" Vanna said slowly watching Soliel as she kept up her prancing and twirling.

"We're the Guardians," Chance said defensively, his eyes following Soliel. They were all doing that, and in doing so, they had to keep moving themselves or else Soliel would get out of their sight. This was something none of them wanted to chance; they were afraid she would disappear if they didn't keep her in their sight.

Soliel's melodic laughter flowed around them as she hopped up on a stump, standing on one foot while the other moved to the music she was still playing.

They just stared at her not sure how to answer. She almost sounded amused, something they surely weren't. Aggravated, now that was close.

"They are calling the children of the Paladins Guardians?" Soliel mused, her voice one of wonderment and amusement. "Seems the Gods do have a sense of humor." Jumping off the stump she twirled around, and the air filled with bubbles that resembled musical notes, all shiny and colorful.

"Look!" Tia gasped.

The bubbles that were floating around them had images inside of them. They moved closer to see if they could tell what the images were but if they accidentally touched a bubble, it would burst.

Paladin? Isn't that what Kull was called? Tia asked looking at the others who gave looks of agreement without making it obvious they were speaking telepathically.

Yeah, but let's not give away what we know just yet. Besides, maybe she'll give us answers that no one else will. They agreed with I.Q. who decided to play ignorant.

"Who are the Paladins?" I.Q. asked. "And why is calling us Guardians humorous?" They could hear the indignation in his voice. The indignation was lost on Soliel who still danced and played her Violin.

Telara glanced over at Cameron and the other Alaskans curious as to what their reaction to this was, but they were just staring at Soliel in amazement. Telara wasn't even sure they were listening to the conversation. Gage, on the other hand, was watching them, his eyes very sharp.

Telara swallowed hard. Coming to Alaska was actually supposed to be a mini vacation for them; instead, they had this.

"One shall become undone," Soliel sang softly, as indifferent to the looks of amazement and awkwardness as she was to I.Q.'s indignation. It seemed she cared nothing for what others thought. She began twirling around as the notes started to glow in the air around them, and the images they had seen earlier became sharper.

In one close to Telara she could see what looked like ancient warriors fighting; their armor looked like a cross between medieval and sci-fi. It was like something you would see at a Comic Con.

As Soliel sang, the images changed. Some of the images looked familiar to them but just as they looked more closely, the image would change.

"Two shall being anew,

Three shall be set free,

Four will unlock the door,

Five will come alive,

Six will try to fix."

She sang the words slowly getting closer to them, dancing and swaying, but they were more interested in the notes that were playing the movies. Telara was sure in one of those images she saw not only Lucius but Kull as well. The others nodded in agreement with her thoughts. Soliel stopped right in front of Telara still playing.

"But it will be the seven that bring the final haven."

Her words tapered off, but the violin kept playing; they could all feel the sorrow in the melody.

"Nice song, but what does that have to do with the Shadows and Darrold?" Gage interrupted, and Soliel twirled in place to look him over. "No disrespect intended," he amended quickly.

Soliel grinned. "The story of the Paladins and their children has everything to do with the Shadows." She started twirling in spot, the notes around her moving faster and faster. "The story that was told is nothing more than a lie to save pride and hide the truth of the horror that happened. It is the story that is untold that will save us all."

Telara looked at her friends; they all agreed that they wanted to know more about the Paladins and these lies

Soliel spoke of. They wanted to know more than any-thing. But they also needed to know how to save Darrold.

"I want to know the truth," Telara told Soliel who gave a very smug smile to Gage. "But they are right, we need to save Darrold right now. If the Shadows are able to get her to awaken the giantess and control the giant-ess, we are in great danger. Everyone." She only prayed that she could get the other answers after they had res-cued Darrold.

Soliel just shook her head. Her look implied she thought Telara a silly little girl. "If you don't know what truly happened, how are you to stop history from repeat-ing itself?"

Between Zach and Soliel, Telara was going to end up with a major headache, but it sounded as if Soliel might actually tell her the story whereas Zach was al-ways so vague. Looking around, she sighed. Right now, they needed to save Darrold.

"How can the story help us find Darrold? We need to save her and keep the giantess asleep."

The notes floated around them as Soliel continued to play her violin. The music was getting faster causing the notes to swirl just as fast. "Only the Paladins can help you."

"How do we find the Paladins?" Telara asked her. They had found one, but they hadn't even been looking for him.

"Names hold the power."

Telara frowned. Wasn't that what Aphrodite had told them back on the island? "Names?"

Like I did back on the island when I said Kull's name while touching the fire emblem; it broke the curse. They didn't need Cole's reminder; that day was still fresh in all their minds.

"The Guardians must give names to those whose names have been taken from them."

Telara was really beginning to wish they had decided to stay back at Sanctuary with Pam. Anything had to be less aggravating than this.

"How do we give names to people we don't know how to find?" Chance's irritation mirrored her own.

Soliel didn't pause in her dancing or her playing. "To find the Paladins you must right a wrong that was done long ago and give those who have no names a name." As she spoke, the notes moved to swirl around her dancing body. Once her last word was spoken, she and her silver notes disappeared.

"Where did she go?" Cameron looked around his expression still one of awe.

"Was she even here?" Tia shoved at Cole calling him an idiot. "What?"

"Not funny."

Tia glared at Cole.

"Who said I was joking?" he protested.

"Who are these Paladins that she spoke of?" Nat interrupted, something that was probably a good thing before another Tia vs. Cole battle broke out.

"Wish we knew," I.Q. said still staring at the spot where Soliel had disappeared. It wasn't that they were trying to be purposely obtuse; they didn't exactly know who the Paladins were. Kull didn't stay around long enough to tell them anything, and Lucius never tells them everything.

None of them knew how to process what they had

just learned. The feeling of being lost out at sea without a life jacket was starting to become common, which
Telara didn't like one bit. She liked knowing what was
going to happen but ever since the first day they had
stepped out of that limo at Sanctuary, she didn't know
what was going to happen from one minute to the next.

"It's late," Nat said, interrupting their thoughts.
"Maybe some sleep would help."

"Yeah, maybe our heads will be a bit clearer tomorrow," Cameron said, but his voice didn't hold the conviction of his words.

Outside her room, the merpeople were patrolling all
decked out in armor with their weapons at the ready.
At first, it took some getting used to having glass walls
separate them from the ocean around them but after just
a few days, it seemed almost natural. Telara watched as
some mermen swam by with what looked like a couple
big orange fish following them. The fish were the size of
a medium dog with fins that looked like spikes.

"They are rather ugly creatures, aren't they?"

She jerked around and saw Zach standing there
watching the same mermen with fish swimming by. He
didn't turn to look at her, just stared through the glass
walls at the sight outside her room.

Would Zach tell her about the Paladins when no one
else would? Sometimes, he could be so helpful but other
times, he could be just as annoying as everyone else.

As if he heard her thoughts, he turned around and
smiled at her.

"Am I sleeping?"

She felt silly asking, but she didn't remember falling asleep and while she did see him that one time when she was awake, they never truly spoke to each other unless she was sleeping.

"You tell me."

She tossed back the covers, jerking herself out of bed in agitation.

"I'm getting tired of all these riddles and mysteries."

"Are you sure about that?" She frowned at him. "Soon enough there will be no mysteries and riddles. You might miss it."

"How could you think that?" She was confused by his response. "Right now, all we're doing is walking around blindly. How could that be a good thing?"

He gave a shrug. "Maybe it's me; I might be the one to miss all the mystery."

"You're confusing me."

She moved to stand by him looking out at the night-time activity. Was it still night? She knew up above the surface it would be bright out no matter the time, but down below the water it was always dark.

The mermen in their armor swimming around with such serious expressions was a great contrast to Bromhilda and her sisters that swam in the lake outside their home in Sanctuary. These were warriors and majestic looking ones at that.

Zach sighed. "I truly am sorry; I wish I could help you more than I have."

"I don't get why no one can come right out and tell us what we need to know." She grimaced. "I mean, seriously? Why does everything have to be a total mystery?"

"Have you thought that maybe it's 'cause it might be

too much for you to take in all at once?" Zach smiled at her, but she wasn't in the mood to be charmed.

"Oh, and us finding out in one summer that we have powers and a destiny that could end in our death isn't too much to take in?" Her retort was sarcastic, and she refused to apologize for it.

"Touché." He grinned at her.

"You know for only learning the American language last year you're doing pretty good," she grumbled.

He laughed. "You're an excellent teacher."

She really didn't want to be complimented; she wanted answers. However, she wasn't sure she would get any from him, even if he were more forthcoming than Lucius who claims to be bound by a promise. They still seemed to learn more from others or on their own.

"What do you know of the Paladins?" She kept her tone neutral even though deep inside she was a tangled mass of nerves waiting for his answer.

"The Paladins?" His look was one of surprise as he turned to look at her. "How did you hear about them?"

"So, you do know who they are?" She grabbed onto his arm in excitement. She truly hadn't expected him to know anything or at least to let her know if he did. While he had been more informative than most, she still felt as if he was holding information back from her. "You have to tell me."

For the first time that she could remember since they first met, his expression became wary. He looked away from her and stared out the glass wall.

"Please, don't shut down on me."

She was still holding onto his arm trying to get him to look at her. She was so close to getting an answer on something; it was right there in front of her. She couldn't let him go.

He turned to look at her, and his expression was one of deep regret.

"I'm sorry."

Then he disappeared right in front of her.

"No!"

Her hand was there holding onto air, and Zach was gone along with her hope to find answers.

Chapter 10

"He just disappeared on you?"

Cole was so distracted that he didn't see the water ball that Chance sent his way until it was too late. The water ball sent Cole flying where he landed in a puddle on the ground, completely wet. Fortunately, it didn't take Cole long to dry out his clothes.

Telara moved swiftly to avoid a snowball that Chad sent her way before responding, "That's what I said."

They met Paul and Wes at breakfast who invited them to join them for some training down in the Coral room. The Coral room was where they did training and exercises Gage told them as they followed the two down the aquarium hallways.

At first, they did hand to hand combat and then some weapon training. Wes showed them how to use their body mass to their advantage while Paul showed them that size doesn't always matter.

"Talk about an oxy-moron," Vanna grinned as they watched and then winced when Paul took a guy that was twice his size down. He flipped him right over his shoulder, and the guy landed with a big thud on his back.

Paul winked at Vanna whose face grew warm as she realized he had heard her.

"Ooohhhh," Cole and Chad both teased with big grins before they were wrestling with some algae and seaweed that came alive. This was the start of the power wars they were now having.

"So not only do we have no answer as how to save Darrold, but we have no answer to who these Paladins are?" The frustration in Chad's voice mirrored the feelings of them all.

"Guardians having issues?" Wes asked as he and Paul took a break from their sparring in the training room.

"Big time," Chad groused as he froze the water ball his brother sent his way, turning it into an ice ball then sending it towards Cole who used his heat to make steam.

"Seems there is an unseen force that just doesn't want us to find any of the answers except the ones they want us to know," I.Q. muttered shocking Vanna's vine that she had twirling up around his legs.

"Really?" Wes and Paul looked at each other; their expression resembled the same looks they would see on Cole and Chad when they were up to no good.

Telara called for a break in the training, and Gage gave her a funny look. He had been the one to remind them that very morning that due to the Shadow troubles, they had been remiss in their training. She motioned for him to come over so he could hear. Turning to Wes and Paul, she asked,

"So, what is on your minds?"

"What makes you think anything is on our minds?" Wes grinned at her.

"We know that look; we have two of our own troublemakers," Tia said motioning towards Cole and Chad who frowned at her.

"Did you hear what she called us brother?" Wes looked at Paul who was grinning.

"I think she called us troublemakers, bro," Paul replied. "I'm not sure whether I am insulted or flattered." The two gave grins that belied their words.

"Brother?" Chad frowned looking between the two. Wes, who had to stand a good foot taller than Paul, looked back at him.

"Yeah."

Don't say it, Chad. Telara stared at him speaking directly to him, but it was too late. Chad was already speaking, leaving them bracing for the backlash.

"What? Are your parents a bear and a dwarf?"

They held their breaths as they waited for either Wes or Paul to knock him on his ass. After all, they had just seen Paul take down a guy who was twice his size.

To their surprise, both Wes and Paul burst out laughing. Vanna walked over to Chad, punched him in the arm, and called him an idiot, causing the two to laugh even harder.

"Ouch! What?" Chad looked at her with a puzzled expression while rubbing his arm.

Vanna opened her mouth, and they all knew she was about to lay into him when Wes grasped Chad's shoulder in his tight grip. Vanna's eyes grew large, probably expecting what the rest of them were: for Wes to toss Chad across the room. Instead, Wes chuckled and said,

"Don't worry about it, bro."

"Don't say it, Chad," his brother warned him.

Paul was laughing at them. "You guys are hilarious."

"Thanks," Telara told him sarcastically. "Just how we want to be seen."

"Nothing wrong with being funny, sweetness." Wes winked at her.

"So, back to what was on your mind," Tia interrupted them, her frustration evident in her voice.

"Sorry, guys." Yeah, Paul didn't truly sound very repentant. "You guys were talking about someone keeping you from finding answers, right?"

They nodded at him.

"Well, we know someone who has answers that no one else has." Wes grinned at them.

"What kind of answers?" I.Q. looked extremely interested. I.Q. wasn't used to being confused but ever since last year, that had been a constant state for all of them.

"Wes," Gage spoke up, his voice full of caution. However, Wes wasn't listening to him.

"Hey dude, they are looking for answers and maybe we can help them find them." Wes just grinned.

"Or make it worse," Gage told him with a raised brow. His expression was one of skepticism, but they were already curious.

"Can't make it worse than it already is," Telara told him and then turned to Wes and Paul. "We would like to meet this someone."

Gage sighed but didn't protest anymore as they followed Wes and Paul out of the Coral room.

"Big Time!" Wes's voice boomed causing I.Q. to flinch.

They stared in disbelief as the big burly Wes grasped hands with another guy who was anything but big. He and Paul looked as if they could be brothers. Wes turned around and grinned.

"Guardians: meet Big Time."

Big Time gave a nod to them and held out his hand. "Heya, glad to meetcha. The name is Drake but mostly I go by Big Time."

Chad was shaking his head with a very perplexed look, and Telara just sighed knowing that whatever was about to come out of his mouth was going to get him slapped by Vanna again.

"Do you Alaskans have any true concept of size?" Chad burst out a bit more loudly than Telara was sure he meant to. His frustration was evident, and she couldn't stop the twitch of her lips. She couldn't help it; sometimes, Chad could be so literal. Usually at the worst times.

"Ow!" He glared at Vanna frowned and smacked him.

"You know, you keep hitting him, and he won't have any marbles left," Paul snickered.

"He lost those long ago," Chance snorted earning him a very rude gesture from his brother who had to duck before Vanna got him again.

Everyone got a laugh at that; well, everyone but Chad that is.

Wes interrupted them before Chad got anymore bruises. "You guys said you needed answers that seemed hidden from you, right?"

Telara nodded, and Wes held his hands out towards Drake. "Well, meet our own secret keeper."

Drake frowned. "Wes..." His tone was cautious.

"Man, it's the Guardians. The Guardians need our help," Wes told him turning to Paul. "Tell 'em, bro."

Paul chuckled, "You just did." Then dodged as a big burly fist aimed for his shoulder.

They laughed.

Vanna gave them both a disgruntled look. "Why do guys insist on always hitting each other?"

Everyone laughed at that, except for Vanna who looked very perplexed. She truly didn't understand the irony in her question.

"What?" She frowned at them.

Drake shook his head and gave a wave of his hand. "Follow me but be warned that it might not be exactly what you are looking for."

Telara opened her mouth to ask what he meant, but he was already walking away. With a shrug, they followed him down corridors and stairways that seemed to go deeper into the Sanctuary.

"This is eerie," Cole said as the hallways seemed to be darker the deeper they went. The water in the walls even looked darker, and the fish that swam there could have starred in horror films. Telara was inclined to agree with Cole.

It seemed they had reached their destination at the bottom of the fourth stairway they had walked down; the only problem was they were staring at a wall. Tia remarked on that, but all Drake, Wes, and Paul did was chuckle.

"I don't see anything funny." She frowned at them.

"Watch," Wes told her as Drake walked up to the wall in front of them and waved his hand over it. The wall opened up into a circular doorway.

"There weren't any crystals," Cole whispered, the shock so much that he forgot to even use their mind speak, which came so naturally to them.

Drake grinned. "I don't need no stinking crystals."

He spoke in a very badly imitated Mexican accent.

"But you always need crystals to open doorways and such." A very confused Cole looked at the rest of them. "Right?"

"Man, you need to get out more," Paul shook his head as he walked through the doorway and disappeared.

They looked at each other and then over at the smiling Wes and Drake. Wes tipped an imaginary hat at them before ducking down and disappearing through the doorway.

They looked at Gage, but he just grinned before following both Wes and Paul. Tia gripped Telara's arm in a bruising grip.

"Ouch!" Telara frowned at her.

"Sorry." She let go but didn't move towards the doorway.

Drake looked at her. "Welcome to my parlour said the spider to the fly." He gave her a wicked grin showing shiny white teeth.

"Not amused." Her arms crossed, and she gave him a hard stare.

"Look, you guys were the ones who wanted to come into our den, not the other way around," Drake told her with raised brows.

She took a deep breath. "Big time," she said with a shrug as she walked through the doorway.

"Now you got it." Drake's booming laughter followed her into the room.

Chapter 11

There wasn't anything significant about the room they walked into unless you counted the fact that the walls were pure darkness with floating lights creating light in the room. There were no swimming fish or merpeople to see.

"Where are we?" Telara looked over at Drake who was watching them with amusement.

"You are in one of the many hidden rooms along the eternal hallway," Wes informed them.

"Eternal hallway?" I.Q. looked perplexed. "How can a hallway be eternal?"

"Let's just say anyone that has attempted to find the end of this hallway has yet to return." Paul shrugged with a sly grin. "So, it has been called the eternal hallway. Not many come down here."

"Makes it the perfect hideaway," Drake said proudly then looked over at Gage who was standing there silently with a stern look on his face. With that look they had a feeling there was a lot more to this than just this one secret society. Drake looked back at them. "Haven't you guys ever wondered about what you were told about Sanctuary and the Arions that lived there? Ever wondered about the story of the Guardians?"

Cole snorted. "Like daily."

"Well, you aren't the only ones."

That got their attention.

"We thought we were the only ones, that everyone else was content with doing what they were told," Tia said leaning against a glass table along the glass wall.

Drake grinned at her. "You were wrong, pretty lady."

Cole's eyes narrowed.

Wes and Paul both snickered at the exchange.

"In every Sanctuary there is a secret few of us who question the story of the Guardians and the Gods."

Wes and Paul joined them at the table. Telara looked over at Gage who gave a nod.

"You mean a secret society within a secret society?" Cole's eyes grew large. "What do you guys call yourselves?"

Wes, Drake, and Paul looked at Cole with curious expressions.

Frowning, Tia nudged Cole.

"Every secret society has a cool name," he protested then grumbled, "Or they should."

"Just call us Sire and bow as we walk by, that is all."

Wes was holding the collar of his T-shirt with both hands and puffing out his chest. Paul, on the other hand, was doing his best to not laugh and failing.

"A curtsy or two might get you a royal hand wave," Paul joked and dodged Wes who tried to hit him, but you could see by the smile on Wes's face it was meant in good fun.

"What is it with guys and having to hit or slug one another?" Vanna groused.

Cole looked at Vanna, then at Tia before looking back at Vanna with a pointed look. Vanna shrugged.

"You bring that on yourself."

Cole opened his mouth then shut it thinking better of whatever it was he was going to say.

"That is probably the first smart thing you have done since I have met you."

Cole frowned at Drake who didn't even seem to notice.

"A.S.S.S.!" Chad shouted, and they turned to look at him frowning.

"The acronym." He grinned, but none of them was sure where he was going with this. However, by the grin on Cole's face, he seemed to get it. Go figure.

"Acronym?" Telara looked at I.Q. who was shaking his head. "Been tutoring them again?"

The gesture Chad sent her way wasn't very polite.

"Okay, so what is ass an acronym for?" Vanna quickly asked Chad before they had an impromptu training match which would include Chad being stuck on the ceiling for hours.

"Alaskan Sanctuary Secret Society." He grinned proudly, and Cole nodded in agreement.

"We'll pass," Drake said dryly.

Ignoring the proud look on Cole and Chad's faces, Telara turned to Drake. "So, what is the story of the Guardians and the Arions?" Her curiosity couldn't be contained any longer. "Since we became Guardians, it seems all we ever find is more questions and not enough answers. The ones who know the answers say they want to help us; yet, they don't tell us anything other than we train, we fight, and we die."

Wes winced at her tone, and she sighed. "Sorry."

"Hey, you have every right to feel the way you do," Paul told her, and Wes nodded along with Drake.

"So, does that mean you will tell us everything?"

"We will tell you what we know, which isn't everything, but more than what is being spread," Drake informed them and after a brief hesitation, they nodded. "There are two reasons that no one will tell you anything. One: they don't know or two: they know and are unable to tell you."

"But why?" Vanna asked from her seat.

"Power." Wes shrugged. "The ones with the knowledge have the power."

"Not only that," Paul grunted. "Also because the ones hiding it from us mere mortals are doing it to cover up something they did."

"Who is trying to hide it?" Chance asked.

"The Gods and Goddesses, who else?"

Everyone turned around startled as a loud voice boomed from behind them. There stood a very tall and beefy guy with thinning blond hair and a smirk on his face. Telara's first thought was, "Here comes trouble."

"Dominic!"

Wes and Paul grinned as their friend joined them, clasping their hands and calling them brother as well.

"Surprised they don't call him Shrimpy," Chad muttered to Cole. "These Alaskans need their vision checked."

Telara was glad that either the trio were ignoring the two or didn't hear them. When they were done with their greetings, Dominic turned and introduced himself.

He cut Telara off before she could introduce themselves to him. "I know who you guys are; all of the Arions do. Don't matter what Sanctuary we are from."

"So, you are saying the Gods and Goddesses are the

ones who are trying to hide the truth from us? Because of something they did?" Telara frowned.

Drake held up his hand stopping Dominic who was about to go into more detail. "We don't have positive proof of that, but we're pretty sure."

Dominic grunted. "Who else would it be? Like you said, it would take someone with a lot of power to pull it off and actually change history books to suit their own needs."

"You have proof that the history books in Sanctuary have been altered?" I.Q. frowned at his words.

Out of all of the Guardians, they knew I.Q. was having the hardest time with everything. He was their mad scientist who never believed in anything he couldn't see. Even though he could see all the mythics and other magical creatures, they were part of the minority with no way to prove it to the world without putting their friends in danger.

"You guys are proof the history books have been altered."

They turned around as another person appeared.

Some secret.

Telara nodded with Tia, people seemed to come out of the woodwork...errr...glasswork. She could hear the other's snickers in her head as she looked at the glass walls around them.

The girl didn't even reach Drake's shoulder as she stood next to him and looked at them with interest.

Feel like a bug under a microscope?

Tia gave a very slight nod in agreement but not enough to alert the other Arions to their private conversation. The newcomer looked like a little pixie, with the haircut to go along with it. Her brown hair was wavy with streaks of lighter color through it. She had on jean shorts, a flannel shirt, work boots, and a leather tool belt around her waist.

"Meet Patches, our fix it all here at Sanctuary," Paul told them grinning as Patches turned her gaze to him but only momentarily before looking back at them.

"So, what do you mean we are proof?" Vanna asked, her tone a bit more defensive than the others were used to hearing.

"You are here, aren't you?" Patches countered back, her face still as she stared back at Vanna.

This could get ugly and fast.

The others nodded to Chance's silently spoken words; Vanna was the sweetest of them all but not when she was upset.

"What does that mean?"

"Do you read any of the history books?" Patches raised a brow, and they could feel the heat rising from Vanna.

"What Patches is so eloquently trying to say while pushing what buttons she can," Drake said, patting Patches on the head as if she was a child, "is that according to the history books the Guardians were tied to one Sanctuary. They grew up in that one Sanctuary, trained until the day the Magine came and -"

"Went out to defeat the Magine and never return," Telara finished for him to which he nodded then grimaced when Patches stomped her heavy work boot on his sneaker-clad shoe before stalking off.

Telara and the other Guardians were trying to hold back their laughter, but Paul, Wes, and Dominic didn't seem to have that same problem. They laughed and slapped their hands on Drake's back.

"New record! She wasn't even in the room for 15 minutes before you upset her."

"Better pray she doesn't sic her Gremlins on you."

Drake groaned at Paul's words.

"Again," Wes finished between laughing.

"Wait! There are Gremlins here too? Like mischievous destructive Gremlins?" Cole and Chad both looked very interested.

"Don't tell them anything!" Tia spoke up before anyone could answer them causing everyone in the room to start laughing, except for Cole and Chad who looked very disappointed.

"You guys are a trip." Wes was laughing.

Chapter 12

The three stooges, as Telara had come to call them, showed them around the rooms. Just like the hallway, they were endless as well. Telara looked at Wes.

"How do you keep this place hidden from Kayne?" At his perplexed look, she continued. "You did say it was a secret; I would assume it would be from those in charge."

Wes shrugged. "Kayne doesn't try to micromanage anyone. He feels as long as we do our job then what we do in our free time is our business."

"Except when you attempted to make that moonshine still on fox island." Dominic grinned at the memory.

"I can't believe he didn't believe me when I told him that I was just trying to make a water purification for the foxes," Wes protested.

"Might have worked if you actually had any architectural skills," Paul chuckled.

"Or if there were still foxes on the island." Dominic shook his head.

"Who says I was talking about the four-legged foxes?" Wes grinned and high-fived both Dominic and Paul. Telara watched them and couldn't stop herself from grinning as well. The friendship between the three reminded her of her own friendship with her friends.

Tia grinned at her. We got them beat. The others nodded in agreement.

"So, how many rooms are there in this secret level of yours?"

Paul shrugged at Vanna's question. "I don't think we ever really counted them."

They turned to look at Gage who wasn't saying much.

"So, does our Sanctuary have a secret society?" Telara queried.

"There is no secret society," Gage told her and at her disbelieving look, he clarified. "Just a bunch of Arions who want to know the truth and yes, every Sanctuary has them. There is no special group, just a bunch of us looking for the truth."

"Is Pam part of it?" Telara was truly curious about that.

"No, she was always by the book," Gage told them. They nodded, understanding exactly what he was saying.

"Speaking of books."

They turned at Drake's remark.

"We have something to show you. Follow me."

They found themselves in another room, but this one seemed to be in the center of the level. The walls were full of darkness but no balls of light. The only light was from crystal scones along the wall. Tia walked over to the nearest wall to them and placed her hand on the glass while staring at the smoke. As they watched, the smoke started to swirl around making what shapes Tia chose.

"The smoke is to keep any unwanted visitors from seeing anything in this room."

They turned to see Drake leaning against an open doorframe watching them with an amused expression.

Tia backed away from the wall, and the smoke went back to once again moving through the walls.

"Sorry."

Drake shrugged and pulled a tattered leather-bound book from a drawer. He placed it on the table as if it were made of crystal.

"This book has been handed down in my family, and we keep it here in this room so no one can find it."

"That?"

Even Tia didn't elbow Cole. The book looked as if one gust of wind would have the pages flying.

"It may not look like anything special, but we were told the Gods would destroy it if they could." Drake watched them. "It is said it was one of the books banned by the leaders." He stared at the book, "It has been handed down my family line with the warning to keep it hidden."

It must be magic. What else could be holding the pages in there?

Drake gave a snicker at their look of disbelief. "It might not be much to look at, but what it holds inside is more precious than any jewel the gnomes could mine."

"Knowledge." I.Q. stared at the book.

Drake nodded. "Knowledge that the Gods would love to bury in the deepest grave in Tartarus."

I.Q. moved close to the book and when he gently pulled back the tattered cover, his eyes grew large.

"That is the same language that is in my Stargazer."

"Your what?"

Drake frowned as if the name confused him, and they couldn't blame him. He probably had never heard of such a thing. They didn't even know if that was the true name of it. That was just the name I.Q. had given it.

"When we first became Guardians, I found a tablet sort of thing that I call a Stargazer. Its language hasn't been easy to translate, but I have been getting better at it."

"Big time!"

They looked up at him.

"What is it with big time?" Telara finally had to ask. "I thought it was your nickname?"

Drake shrugged. "It is..."

"He also says it for everything!" Patches walked in and while her expression was innocent, they could hear the roll of her eyes in her voice. "Don't ask, just accept it," she told them drolly as she hopped up on the table where the book lay, ignoring the narrowed eyed look Drake gave her.

"So how can some kids who aren't even demi-Gods manage to keep the Gods from finding out about it?" I.Q. asked staring at the book. Telara was surprised he had waited this long to ask that question.

"Who says we aren't demi-Gods?" Drake grinned.

Each of the questions that rose with those words stuck in their throats as bells and alarms went off all around them.

"Shadow attack?"

Chance looked around. Those were the same alarms they heard back at their Sanctuary.

"Well, they ain't singing Dixie," Patches said jumping off the table and heading out the door. The book seemed to have disappeared as well, something Telara could understand. I.Q. was just as protective over his Stargazer.

"Follow us."

Three turns and half a flight of stairs found them back in the main hallway where flannel shirts were running everywhere. They followed Drake and Patches to the Control Room where Kayne was already directing his Arions into suits.

"What's going on?"

They were standing with Drake.

"Shadows attacking the merpeople." Gage was suiting up.

"Dude, you're going too?" Cole stared at Gage who stopped and looked at him.

"He has weapons he can use." Tia shoved Cole in aggravation.

"But under water?"

Tia stopped and looked over at Wes and Paul who were already suiting up.

"Can we use our Crims under water?" she asked.

"Wait! How are we going to fight under water?" I.Q. said.

I.Q. looked at the wall where suited up Arions were already walking through. They watched as they moved through the glass and then started to glide through the water as if it were nothing.

"The pressure and cold alone will kill us," I.Q. informed them.

It was Kayne who answered them. "Your suits will protect you, just like they did when you guys were swimming down your first day here. Before the discovery of the many uses of crystal essence we have now, we had to go out in crystal bulbs."

"Yeah, those things were bulky and a pain to try to

maneuver when battling the Shadows," Patches grumbled as her suit suddenly covered her body. Her face was uncovered, but they knew the suit would still protect her face. She gave a wave as she walked through the wall.

"Your Crims will work just fine," Kayne assured them. "You had better hurry; the others will need your help."

On the screen it looked as if a whale was swimming over the merpeople's palace, but as the screen zoomed in, they could see it was really a Shadow.

"Whoa!" Chad jumped back into his brother who was staring at the screen.

"Okay, guys! We need to do this," Telara told them as she started moving towards the wall taking a deep breath as her suit covered her body. She turned to the others and grinned before walking through the wall.

She felt a chill, probably from the water. She remembered I.Q. saying something about freezing to death, although the water didn't seem that cold to her. She moved her feet along the floor slowly trying to get her bearings.

Hey, slow poke! Let's get a move on.

Chance glided right by her as if he had been born in the water; of course, that wasn't far off for the swimming captain of their high school swim team.

Let's go, T.

With a startled look, she looked up at Wes who was beckoning them forward.

You guys can communicate with us like this as well?

How else are we going to communicate while out here? he quipped with a grin and gestured for them to follow him. Chance, of course, was already swimming into the fray.

Pushing off the floor, Telara willed herself to follow Wes and, to her amazement, she did just that. She looked down and saw the Rotary twinkling on her wrist over the suit.

Maybe this wouldn't be so bad.

A mermaid was fighting with a Shadow that resembled an eel and losing badly. Telara looked to Tia who nodded and pulled out her Crim. Tia started to swirl the whip in the water creating a vortex. Several Arions stopped to watch looking impressed.

Don't let it get too big or you might not be able to control it, Patches' worried voice could be heard. All Telara could think was, "Thank God it wasn't Cole."

No worries, I got this, Tia said then released the small vortex that moved and swept up the Shadow along with a few others in its way. Tia smirked.

Alright guys! Let's clear up the Shadows on the outside so we can join the fight in the kingdom. Gage appeared next to them, crystal bombs attached to his belt and the crystal baton in his hand. They nodded as they took out a few more stragglers.

Could use some light, Chance grumbled as he got knocked over by a Shadow that appeared in the shape of a merman. These stupid Shadows have the advantage.

At least it isn't as cold as I.Q. thought it was going to be. Cole grinned as he used his nunchucks that lit up even while under water. The Shadow creature ran as soon as the water illuminated with its glow.

If it weren't for the suits we are wearing, we would all be dead within 15 minutes, Wes told them as he fired three arrows of light at three different Shadows. He nailed each one, causing them to disappear in puffs of Shadow mist.

But- Vanna started to protest.

We don't have the time to try to detain them, Wes told her. We need to get them out of the merpeople kingdom before they do any more damage. When it looked as if she was going to argue some more, his tone took a harsh turn. They are my friends, too, but right now I have to worry about the ones who aren't trying to kill us!

Wes took off with one mighty kick of his feet heading towards the city. Vanna watched him swim away with a look of regret. Telara put her arm around her.

Come on, Van. We need to get these Shadows out of here before anyone gets seriously hurt.

I just want to help everyone, especially the ones who can't help what they are doing.

With a dejected look, Vanna swam towards the city. They could see flashes of light as Arions did their best to drive away the Shadows that were attempting to abscond with as many merpeople as they could. That was their little Mother Nature: believing she could help everyone and when she found out she couldn't, well, she never did take it well.

So, if the water would kill us in fifteen minutes how do the mermaids survive?

Telara stopped in mid swim at Chad's question. They looked at each other and then towards Patches who was swimming towards them. By the look in her eyes, Telara was sure that she had heard the question.

Are you guys seriously asking stupid questions while our team members are fighting?

Patches swam past them without waiting for an

answer. Telara had to admit that, considering the situation, it was a rather stupid question. With a wave of her hand, they swam quickly after Patches towards the city ahead of them.

Chapter 13

They swam past buildings until they came to the inner city. Telara paused as she stared along with the others at the sight before her. There were many gorgeous buildings that shone brightly in the water Designed with architecture like nothing they had ever seen: glass and a coral molded into works of art that were buildings.

Buildings that were right now taking a beating from the Shadows and Arions fighting.

Let's go.

Telara really wanted to stare and take in the beauty around them, but they didn't have time. With a kick of her feet, she moved forward and let her Rotary glow bright. A few Shadows ran from the glow, but there was one rather large one that resembled a squid who wanted to play.

The tentacles wrapped around her waist and tightened, making it hard for her to breathe. She tried kicking out at the creature, but it evaded each kick. In frustration, she hit it with her fist. The Rotary glowed, and the tentacle let go. A garbled scream could be heard as she kicked away from the creature.

Fried squid on the menu tonight!

Kaleb swam between Telara and the squid, lifting his Crim that turned into a Tommy Gun. He fired off several lighted balls that crackled when they contacted the squid that screamed in pain.

He has a Tommy Gun! Chad stared in amazement and something that was akin to envy. I want one of those! Make that full-blown envy.

Kaleb lifted his Crim up and blew on the metal barrel with a smirk, winking at them before turning and taking aim at other Shadows attempting to steal away any Arion or merperson they could get.

Tia watched Kaleb swim away. She was not paying attention and let one of the squid Shadows get too close. Its tentacles wrapped around her waist, pinning her arms to her sides along with her Crim and leaving her struggling. Paul swam up, and his Crim formed a Scythe; it became a metal handle with grips and a purple crystal blade that slashed through the Shadow's tentacle.

The reaper is in the house! Wes's laughter could be heard as Paul gave them a salute before joining the battle within the kingdom.

Inside the city, it was hard to tell the Shadow creatures from the shadows cast by the buildings. Lights were flashing all around from the Crims, and shrieks could be heard all around them but still they came.

Chance was moving past everyone and everything with the ease of a merman.

Try to keep up, Chance chuckled taking out two Shadows that were pulling a struggling mermaid towards the shadows of the castle. She sent him a grateful smile before swimming off.

Light arrows flew from I.Q.'s bow right past Chance's left ear. Chance's eyes were wide, but the painful scream from the Shadow merman that was about to grab him drowned out what he was about to say.

Times like this I can see the resemblance between you

and your brother. I.Q. kicked off and swam towards the battle ignoring the indignant look from both Chance and Chad.

"Halt, interlopers!"

Turning around, they saw Adrijan there with a lop-sided algae and coral crown on his head that you could tell he had handcrafted. He was holding out a floppy piece of seaweed as if brandishing a sword. His black hair was floating around him as he stared them down.

"You invaders! Prepare to feel my wrath!"

A ball of light flew right by them and exploded just by Adrijan sending several Shadows that were sneaking up on him screaming away. They turned, and there was Kaleb with his glowing Tommy Gun giving them a salute as Paul stood next to him with his glowing Scythe.

"Adrijan, go find somewhere safe. We are trying to get rid of the Shadows." Paul's voice echoed around them, surprising them that he was able to project his voice under the water.

Adrijan looked up at him and gave a regal nod to him. "Very well good, sir. Carry on and take care of these invaders to my land."

With that, he turned around and swam away. They could hear Paul's internal sigh as he swam away from them towards more Shadows. They looked at each other before shrugging and following.

Their suits helped them see under the water but with as many Shadows that were attacking along with the lights the Crims were making, it was very difficult for those not used to fighting like this. It was annoying as well. Telara prayed that no one had been taken, but it was hard to tell. They didn't want to completely harm any of the Shadows knowing they could be innocents or even comrades, and that put them at a great disadvantage.

The bigger disadvantage was Vanna not being able to heal the Shadows even though she was trying. Chad had to freeze a Shadow that managed to wrap its arms around her, pulling her away.

Telara was using her Rotary as a shield and whip against the Shadows attacking her as well as the others. One wrapped his arms from behind her making it hard to hit him with her whip. Struggling only made its grip tighten. She felt herself being pulled away and saw that her friends who were attempting to swim towards her were being overwhelmed by the Shadows.

She was on her own. Another Shadow appeared before her. Raising her arm, she struck out with a light whip causing the Shadow to shriek and swim away from the light. Every attempt to swing the whip to hit the one pulling her down was thwarted by a new Shadow. She felt like she was battling a stupid hydra right now.

She grew frustrated, doing her best to keep the Shadows from her and struggling against the Shadow pulling her closer to the shadow on the sound floor.

A knife would be helpful right now, she thought raising her arm and ready to hit out at more Shadows. To her surprise, instead of the long whip a very sharp looking blade grew from the Rotary.

The sound floor was getting closer, and she knew once they got her into that shadow she would be lost from her friends. She wasted no time in raising her arm and bringing the blade down into the arm of the creature pulling her. With that thrust, a painful scream blasted all around her, and she felt herself being shoved away from the shadows.

She hit the wall of the nearest building to her with enough force that the wall cracked. Everything around her started to glow. She looked up and saw everyone was looking down at her wrist. Her Rotary was glowing more brightly than she had ever seen it.

Screams could be heard as Shadows started to run away from the light for not only was her Rotary glowing, but the building was as well and not only that building, but the whole city seemed to start glowing.

What is going on?

Telara looked up to see Cameron staring at her Rotary, the start of the light show.

I don't know. Which she didn't.

Vanna swam to her quickly as the Shadows started to flee, her Crim in relax form and wrapped around her hand. Vanna pressed her hand against the Rotary before Telara could stop her. Telara didn't know what was happening, and the thought of her Rotary hurting Vanna was too much. The second the Crims touched, the light started to get a green hue about it.

They looked up and gasped in shock. The Shadows that the light touched were glowing and then healing. Confused merpeople were staring about them along with some other creatures as well.

Get them transported to the Sanctuary immediately! Cameron was shouting.

Transport the merpeople? That confused Telara until she realized some of the healed Shadows were actual people. People that weren't in any types of suits to protect them from the water around them. The Arions moved quickly, and the people started disappearing until the only ones left in the city were the Arions in their suits, the Guardians, and the merpeople.

What was that? Wes and Paul joined them with the other Arions following.

Telara shrugged and laughed. Vanna always finds some way to get her way.

She looked around them at the buildings, curious about what the mermaids used to build their homes.

Either that or we never hear the end of it until she does. Cole grinned and dodged behind Chance really quickly when Vanna swirled around in the water to glare at him.

Think you can do some of that magic and help clean up the city? Patches joined them.

Telara gave a shake of her head. We aren't even sure how we did that, sorry.

Come on, guys! Let's get this cleaned up, so we can head back to Sanctuary.

They swam to start helping the merpeople clean up the mess left by the Shadow attack.

All the Factions pitched in to help with the clean-up, even Shayne could be seen picking up small pieces of rubble and tossing them into a coral bucket located nearby. Arions and merpeople were working side by side cleaning up the streets. Telara grinned at her friends. It was nice to see teamwork such as this.

Telara picked up a piece of a building and was about to toss it into a bucket when it started to glow. She turned and stared at her friends who were looking just as startled; the pieces in their hands were glowing as well. She looked around them, closed her eyes, and tried to let the magic flow. She could feel the others following suit, could feel the combination of their powers.

They heard gasps all around them. Opening their eyes, they saw the kingdom lit up once more. This time, they focused their thoughts on cleaning and repairing the city. As they watched, the rubble disappeared, and the buildings repaired themselves. Telara caught Patches looking at her, and she gave a helpless shrug. She had no idea how she did it, but she knew it had something to do with the buildings.

The King approached them cautiously, keeping his eyes on Telara and her friends. "We thank you for your help but now we must insist that you leave so that we can attend to our injured."

Before they could protest or say anything, Cameron swam between them and the King giving a solemn nod of his head. "Yes, Your Majesty." He turned and raised his hand towards Sanctuary.

Let's head home.

But we need to know what their buildings are made of, Telara protested. We have never had our powers amplified like that.

Cameron shook his head and motioned for everyone to leave. They won't tell anyone and if we don't leave, we chance starting a battle we won't win. When it looked as if Telara and the other Guardians were about to argue, Cameron spoke more sharply. This isn't your Sanctuary; the same rules don't apply here.

With a disgruntled look back at the city where they could already see merpeople quickly disappearing into the buildings and the royal guard assembling, they took off towards Sanctuary.

Chapter 14

"You wouldn't let me ask him anything!" Telara whirled on Cameron as soon as they entered the Command Center.

"You're right." Cameron turned to Nat. "Have all the wounded been tended to?" When she nodded, he turned to everyone else. "Take care of your equipment and get your rest."

He turned to Shayne who was still in her suit. Telara didn't even remember seeing her out in the battle. Of course, she had to admit, it wasn't like it was easy to tell who all was out there.

"Shayne, you will need to add extra patrol around the Command Center and the mermaid kingdom along with all the villages on the islands."

Shayne's eyes flashed, and Telara was sure she was about let him have it with her words when Kayne interrupted.

"He's right, Shayne. Something is going on and after what happened out there, the Shadows are surely going to want to stop us."

"We freed th-" Vanna started to protest, but Kayne stopped her with a raise of his hand.

"I'm not saying you did anything wrong, just that we need to be prepared for the fallout."

Vanna didn't look soothed by any means, but Kayne

had already turned to start delegating orders, and everyone was moving to follow them.

They stood there feeling very out of sorts and not knowing exactly what they should do.

"Come on, I'll walk you guys back to your rooms and see if I can answer your questions that you have," Cameron said softly to them. "All of you look tired and about ready to drop; you need your sleep, and I know you won't sleep without some answers. Just be prepared to not like the answers you get."

Some answers are better than none.

Telara nodded at Tia's words as they followed Cameron down the halls towards their rooms.

"Do you know what the buildings are made of?" Telara asked him.

Cameron shook his head. "No idea."

"Why wouldn't you let us ask him?" She really couldn't understand that. It was an innocent question, wasn't it?

Cameron took a deep breath. "This isn't your Sanctuary," he started, but Telara interrupted him.

"Yeah, we know." She tried not to sound to irritated, but they were all getting sick of not knowing what was going on.

Cameron stopped and turned to them. "No, you don't. In the lower 48, the rules are different than they are in Alaska. We don't govern the mythicals that live here like your Sanctuary does. Here, we coexist with many of them, but we also answer to them."

"Answer to them?"

For once no one hit, shoved, or shushed Cole. They had never heard of answering to the mythicals; Telara couldn't even imagine Ira letting the pixie King and Queen speak to him the way they spoke to Kayne.

Not in Kansas anymore, Dorothy.

They ignored Chad's mental quip.

"Back home, the mythicals need us for their protection," Gage appeared behind them. "You have to search four hours or more to find even a small patch of wilderness while in Alaska, it's everywhere."

"We could spend hours and days discussing the difference between Alaska and the lower 48," Cameron told them. "But the bottom line is that the mythicals lived here in Alaska long before any humans came to this land. They are the true natives, and they don't let any of us here at Sanctuary forget that. We are only allowed here by their grace, which can be revoked at any time with a unanimous vote by the ruling tribes."

"The Sanctuary leaders agreed to that?" Chance asked while the rest of them were silent trying to process all they were hearing. This was truly different than anything they had ever heard before.

"They didn't have a choice; the Shadows are the only reason the mythicals allowed a Sanctuary to be built here." Cameron gave a derisive chuckle. "Many of the tribes consider us to be working for them."

"The mythicals run Sanctuary?" Cole's expression mirrored their own confusion.

"They like to think so." Cameron shrugged. "But even the Tribunal had to agree that it would be a conflict of interest."

"How?" Vanna asked. "If this is their land, why can't they be the ones to call the shots?"

"And exactly which tribe would you suggest run Sanctuary?" Cameron asked her.

"What do you mean?"

"There is more than just one tribe in Alaska. Each of their elders make up the Tribunal that rules all magic in Alaska. When Sanctuary first came here, each chief of their tribe petitioned to be the ones that run Sanctuary, but the Tribunal agreed that not one tribe could run Sanctuary, for they would only think of their own vested interests."

"I still don't understand how that is a conflict of interest."

"Simple, they needed an outside influence that still answered to the Tribunal just as all the tribes did. Even in your world, pixies and fairies don't play well together. Do you really think the pixies would give the fairies the same protection as they would their own village?"

"I didn't think about that," Vanna admitted gnawing on her bottom lip.

"That doesn't mean we still don't answer to them at times. When we are on their home turf, we have to be careful. If we do anything that could potentially violate any of their laws or do anything that conflicts with their beliefs and they take it to the Tribunal who side with them, we could lose everything we have achieved here. We could lose Sanctuary."

"Don't they care that we are here to protect them?" Telara was honestly confused. It sounded as if the mythicals didn't want Sanctuary here, and that she couldn't understand at all.

Cameron sighed. "Many of the mythicals in Alaska are thankful for us, and the elders know they can't defeat the Shadows without us. But they can't argue with tradition and laws that were in place since the beginning of time. The ruling families of each tribe have their own way of ruling their people and as long as we respect that without upsetting the tribes, we can run Sanctuary without any interference."

Cameron turned and started walking down the hall. He turned down the corridor heading to their rooms.

"The ruling families still believe that they should be the ones running Sanctuary and will find any reason to be able to shut down Sanctuary and then petition the Tribunal for ownership." Cameron looked around them before speaking again. "The mermaids have never had a problem coexisting with us, as long as we have kept our distance. They help mine the crystals only because they are unable to harness their power like us, but they are very strict that no outsiders are allowed in their kingdom except in cases like today."

"What would they get out of shutting Sanctuary down?" I.Q. looked perplexed. "As you said, they can't harness the powers of the crystals like we can."

"The merpeople know and understand that, but the other tribes feel that we are hiding things from them. However, without the sanction from their Tribunal, they can't do anything, so we do our best to not give them any cause to take to the Tribunal."

"We're missing something here," Tia spoke up just as they reached their rooms. She looked at Cameron. "There has to be something behind this animosity when Sanctuary is here to protect them."

Cameron looked at Gage who nodded at him with an expression of unease. Cameron turned to look at them.

"Sanctuary, every Sanctuary, was created to protect the magical community from the Shadows. Your Sanctuary was the first to start governing the mythicals they were tasked with protecting."

Telara looked over at Vanna whose brow was already furrowed. Oh boy.

"Before you go all righteous anger on Ira," Gage said to Vanna who didn't look very receptive. "It was before his time and, unlike Alaska, the lower 48 don't have the wilds where mythicals can roam without man, or woman," he added quickly when Vanna raised a brow at him. Cole and Chad sniggered. "The mythicals in our Sanctuary came there of their own free will, finding it hard to live amongst the mortals."

"I doubt they asked to be repressed," Vanna griped still not looking appeased by his explanation. "Bet if they had the opportunity to come here and live, they would do it in a heartbeat."

"And you would lose that bet," Gage replied.

Vanna snorted at Gage's words.

"Here, they would have to follow the rules of the ruling family and not many want to that."

"So, what's the difference between that and having to follow the rules of Sanctuary?" Vanna wasn't letting it go.

"At least in Sanctuary when they break the rules, they can still live their lives."

Gage turned and walked away from them to his room. He opened the door, looked in, and then looked back at them.

"Nothing is black and white; even the worst person can have the best intentions. The one thing that always stays the same is the fact that you have to respect the laws of others even if it doesn't fit into what you think it should be."

With that said, he walked into his room and shut the door.

"Well, night, I guess." Cameron hurriedly went back down the hall leaving them standing there outside their rooms.

"So where does this leave us?" Vanna asked, breaking the silence that remained after Cameron's hasty departure. "Without being able to find out what those buildings are made out of, how are we going to find out what gave us that magnification of our powers?"

"Yeah, that could be what we need to defeat the Shadows. You would think they would want that." Cole glowered out the glass walls where the merpeople kingdom could just be seen in the distance.

"What if that is the only way I'll be able to heal the Shadows from now on?"

Vanna was starting to get agitated and started pacing. Telara knew she hated the fact that she couldn't heal the Shadows back at Darrold's. They worried about that. They had come to depend on Vanna and her healing ability to give them a big advantage in the battlefield. Without Vanna and her ability to heal the Shadows, they were pretty much back to square one.

Vanna kicked the wall and fell back against the glass muttering, "They could've parted with just one lousy piece. What would it have hurt?"

Chance looked at Vanna his brow furrowed. "What?" she asked feeling agitated.

Chance shrugged his shoulders as he shook his head. "Sorry, Van. But I expected you to tell us that we should respect their wishes."

"Well, nothing we can do about it now," Telara said quickly before their Mother Nature, who always stood up for those who couldn't, lost her temper, something every one of them never liked to see. Staring at her door, she could feel the fatigue from the day starting to catch up on her.

"Who says?"

They turned to look at I.Q. who had a Cheshire grin on his face.

"I've seen that smile before!" Tia started to grin. "What did you do I.Q.?"

He shrugged, just barely pulled his hand from his pocket, and opened it just a bit, enough that they could see the sparkling texture of the rock in his palm. They gasped as he hurriedly put his hand back into his pocket.

"You dog!" Cole was grinning and slapping I.Q. on his back. "You outsmarted them all."

"Shhhh!" I.Q. frowned looking around. "Not if you let the cat out of the bag I haven't."

"Oh!" Cole put his hand against his mouth looking contrite. "Sorry."

"That's alright. But let's keep this under wraps until we get back home."

They agreed and declared the day was done. They retired to their rooms. They were very tired but now more optimistic about the trip, except for Telara who hoped the nagging feeling she felt had nothing to do with the fact that I.Q. had just stolen from the merkingdom.

Chapter 15

"Hey! Earth to Telly!"

Telara was lost in her thoughts. She didn't see the bagel until it was dangling right in front of her face. She shuddered and looked around confused.

"Good catch, Tia."

Chad looked impressed, but Cole was suddenly trying to look as if he had no idea what was going on, which meant he was the one behind the bagel Tia had just managed to stop from hitting her in the face.

"Grow up!"

Tia glared at Cole and sent the bagel flying back at him. His response was to set it on fire. Chance then shot the water from Cole's drinking glass to put out the fire and in doing so Cole ended up sprayed in the face.

"Hey!" Cole jumped up and glared at the unapologetic Chance.

"Yow!"

They jumped when Chance leaped from his seat, his hand swatting at his backside. The smirk on Cole's face told them all they needed to know.

This was about to turn into another impromptu power battle, and Telara really wasn't in the mood for it. She stood up and slammed her hands on the table.

"Enough!"

Flashes of fire and water could be seen bouncing off

an invisible wall in front of the two. They quickly turned staring at Telara who was just as surprised as they were.

"How did you do that?" Tia was looking impressed, but Telara could only shrug her shoulders. She truly didn't know but was thankful it didn't hurt anyone, just obstructed both Cole's and Chance's powers.

"Is this normal?"

They turned to see Paul leaning against the wall watching them.

"Unfortunately," Telara sighed and sat back down.

"Hey!" Chad protested. "I didn't do anything."

"This time," Tia told them.

Chad opened his mouth, but his words were drowned out by the sirens going off as the alarms sounded.

"What now?" Telara groaned but rose with the rest of them as they raced off to the command room.

As they entered, they saw Gage standing next to Kayne. They were staring at the view screen before them.

"Where is that?" Vanna tilted her head staring at the image of the grassy mountain with trees and water all around it. "It looks vaguely familiar."

"The Sleeping Lady."

They turned to see someone who didn't look like any teenager they had ever met. His long wild hair was pulled back by a leather strap although his hair looked to be about as rebellious and wild as his brown eyes. His rugged green looking pants were tucked into leather boots. He wore a matching green shirt and camo looking jacket. Along with his Crim and other crystal accessories, he had an actual gun in a holster.

"We tracked them to Independence Mine but lost them. By the time we were able to pick up their trail again, they had increased in number at The Sleeping Lady."

Kayne nodded at him. "Thank you, Jesse. You and your team look tired."

"Don't even think you are going to ground my team." Jesse stared at Kayne who looked him over.

Uh-oh, I have seen that look between Ira and Claw before. Vanna nervously chewed on her lip as they waited to see what Kayne would say.

Kayne finally shrugged. "Who am I to argue with your hard head? Just make sure you don't go in unprepared."

Jesse snorted, "As if I would dare to endanger my team in such a way; I ain't no Cheechako."

"Hey!" Cole protested, but no one was paying them any attention as Shayne had gasped bringing their attention back to the view screen.

They saw Darrold standing next to the cloaked female and looking very tired. Black mist was rising all around Darrold, the mist moving along with the cloaked female's hand movements as if she were commanding its movement. She probably was; it wasn't like they truly knew what they were up against.

"Who is that woman?" Shayne asked the question they all had.

"She isn't a traditional Shadow," a boy standing next to Jesse spoke up.

He looked such a contradiction to Jesse. He was Glen, Jesse's second, who had the same height as Jesse but not the bulk and definitely not the hair. He looked young, but he looked as if he was already balding. Tia elbowed Cole before he could say anything; they could hear his thoughts.

"She commands not only the Shadow creatures but shadows as well. She was the reason we lost them at the mines. She created a darkness that even the light from our Crims couldn't pierce."

That sent chills down their spines. They relied on the light from their Crims when fighting the Shadows.

"She was the one who was there when Gage was turned into a Shadow," Telara spoke up, staring at the woman. Everyone looked from her to Gage who was very pale.

"If you can't fight, Gage, we would understand," Beth spoke up kindly. "That can't be something easy to get past."

Gage shook his head. "No, I won't sit this out while you guys fight." Gage was already attaching his belt with the crystal bombs in a bag along with his crystal baton. Telara grinned. She was happy that Gage would be going with them; it wouldn't be the same without him. "Besides, I have some paybacks to deliver."

"Yeah!" Wes, Dominic, and Paul cheered along with the others. "Let's go defeat some Shadows!"

The Guardians frowned looking around them at the Alaskan Arions in jeans and flannels with their crystal Crims.

"What about our suits? Aren't we suiting up before battle?"

Paul just smirked, his Scythe Crim glowed in his hand as he twirled it around. "You're in Alaska now. Time to play by a different set of rules."

"Let's go, reaper!" Wes clapped Paul's shoulder, ambling past him in his jeans and flannel and heading towards the transporters where the others were gathering and disappearing in flashes of light. With a smirk, Paul transformed his Scythe back to the Crim and attached it to the leather belt around his waist.

"Van, you coming?"

Chance's words had them all turning to where Vanna stood as if in a trance.

"Vanna, you okay?"

Telara moved towards her then stopped as a rumbling could be heard from beneath them.

"What was that?"

Telara didn't have an answer for Cole but whatever it was, it was getting nearer.

"Are you guys doing this?" Kayne asked, but they just shook their heads, although...Vanna still hadn't moved. It was as if she was in a trance of some sort; she just stared straight ahead silent and unseeing.

"Van, you okay?"

Telara started to run towards her friend when the ground beneath Vanna's feet opened up and swallowed her in a green bud before disappearing back beneath into the earth.

"Vanna!"

They ran towards where the bud disappeared, but it was too late. Vanna was gone.

The room had gone silent as they stared at the hole where their friend had once stood. No one knew what to say.

"Where did she go?" Cameron looked at them, but they gave a helpless shrug. "Has she ever done that before?"

"No." Telara looked at them. "Never."

"Until now," Cole said still staring at the hole.

"What do we do?" Tia looked at Telara and the others.

Telara closed her eyes. Van! she hollered out hoping that wherever Vanna was she would be able to reach her through their bond.

"What happened?"

Telara opened her eyes to see her friends holding their heads and Kayne giving her a funny look. Telara winced.

"Sorry guys."

"No big deal." Cole shook his head and tapped his ear several times with his palm then looked at her. "Were you able to find her?"

"No." Telara tried to hide the worry she was feeling, but she knew from the looks on the others' faces that she was failing.

"We have to find her." I.Q. walked over to the hole and peered down.

"You guys go find her; we can take care of the cloaked wonder and her Shadow goons." Paul twirled his Crim in his hand until it changed to the glowing purple Scythe.

"All you need is a black cloak, man." Cole looked at him with wonderment, and Paul just sneered.

"The reaper wished he could be me," was Paul's cocky reply.

Telara wanted to go, she really wanted to, but they had no idea where Vanna was, and they knew nothing about this land they were in.

"We can't." Her words were heavy and her eyes bright. "We have to trust that she can take care of herself; we have a duty to stop the Shadows." She swallowed hard, hating herself for what she was saying. "We need to head to The Sleeping Lady with the others."

No one moved from where they stood over the hole.

"We don't know this land; we could spend days looking for her and not find her. Or we can go do the job that we all signed up for and pray that she will be able to take care of herself until we can find her," Telara explained.

Jesse walked over to them and placed his hand on her shoulder. "We'll help you locate her as soon as we secure The Sleeping Lady. You have my word." The whole room murmured their agreement and support.

Cole opened his mouth to argue with Telara. She had no idea if it was the look on her face, what Jesse said, or maybe he just realized that she was right, even if it did suck big time, but he shut his mouth with a nod.

She turned to look at Kayne. "Let's get this done with so we can go find Vanna and take down whoever was foolish enough to take away one of our own."

Kayne nodded, turning to Shayne who wasn't suited up but taking over one of the smaller digital screens where she could see The Sleeping Lady.

"Shayne will stay behind with me and our techs so that we can coordinate through the view screens."

They nodded to Kayne and with one last look back at the hole, they headed towards the transporters.

It was time to save Alaska and the world.

Vanna groaned as she opened her eyes and stared up into the bright sun above her.

"What happened?"

She rolled over and looked for the others, but no one was there but her.

"Where is here? How did I get here?"

She put her hand to her forehead; she felt out of sorts, lightheaded. She pushed herself up on one knee, trying to fight the wave of dizziness that threatened her, and looked around.

She was at Darrold's place. How did she get here? With that one question, it all came rushing back to her. She remembered standing with the other Guardians and getting ready to head to The Sleeping Lady to save Darrold. She was about to follow the others when she heard a voice calling out to her, crying for help. She couldn't see anyone, though. Then she had heard the rumbling from the ground, which had opened beneath her.

The bud that wrapped her in its protective embrace pulled her down into the ground and carried her hundreds of miles through the earth, under the water, the train tracks, and all those mountains. It amazed her now how she could have known exactly where they were as the bud moved. Were her powers growing? Did she summon that bud or did someone else summon her?

She looked around her. Someone walking up to this house would never have known that only days before there had been a great battle here. The vegetable beds with actual metal bedframe headboards were all back in place as well as the flip flops along the fence. The big ball made out of metal barrel rings was also back in its place. Why on earth was she here? Who had brought her here?

"Squawk! I want flowers for the princess! Squawk!"

Vanna looked up to see Nikos flying above her.

"Squawk! Only red petals allowed! Squawk!"

"Nikos?" Could he have summoned her she wondered.

"Squawk! I am a platinum member! Squawk!"

Chapter 16

Walking out of the transporter, they stopped at the sight that greeted them: Darrold was no longer an elderly human but a tiny pixie caught in black smoke. Her eyes were glowing an eerie white as she hung in the air above the mountain. The woman in the cloak was standing on a huge rock formation at the base of the mountain with Shadow creatures of all kinds surrounding her.

There were the minions they were all used to seeing all over the mountain side, their clawed hands moving with their bodies as they prowled restlessly. The bigger generals were standing still waiting for commands. Then there were the shapeshifting Shadows that were changing their shapes from animals, mythicals, and then even to the form of humans. All stood between them and Darrold.

"We need to get to Darrold before she wakes Susitna," Cameron said as he moved forward. With a flick of his wrist, his Crim extended like a staff but one with a sword at the end and with very intricate designs. He started to twirl the staff in his hands.

"Got any plans? I am all ears," Cecil said as he grabbed his Crim with both hands and pulled them apart creating two bad ass looking brass knuckles with blades arcing over them.

Paul moved forward with his Scythe, and the other

Arions pulled out their Crims into weapon form.

"Don't die." Cameron shrugged.

"Seriously? That's your advice?" Cole stared at him, his nunchucks hanging from his hands.

"Seems like solid advice to me," Lyla said as her staff extended from her Crim.

"Big time!" Drake grinned as his Crim just disappeared.

"Dude, where did your Crim go?" Chad asked.

Drake grinned at him and showed him the Chinese throwing stars in his hand.

"Wicked," Chad breathed.

"Focus everyone! We need to take these guys down and get Darrold safe and sound before we can go find our missing comrade," Jesse spoke up, holding a very wicked machete knife in his hand, made of crystal and metal of course.

"He's right! Let's get this finished so we can find Van," Telara said, trying to choke down the emotion at hearing them calling Vanna a comrade. There may be a lot of things in Alaska that she didn't understand, but the connection and closeness between those in Sanctuary she truly got.

The cloaked woman laughed. "You actually think you can defeat me and my Shadows? Silly children. When the giant awakens without her love here, you will discover the meaning of true agony." She raised her arm, and the Shadows leapt through the air towards them. "Attack, my Shadows!"

"Remember, our goal is to get Darrold!" Lyla shouted as she leaped over a Shadow and did a twist in air while swinging her glowing staff to connect with the Shadow's legs, bringing it down with a wail.

"Sure, will get right on that," Wes said as he stopped and took aim at two Shadows who were sneaking up on Dominic as he battled one of the shapeshifting Shadows. They screamed in pain as the light arrows found their mark.

"Got your back brother!" Then he jumped when a Shadow wailed from behind him as Paul's Scythe went flying through the air creating a purple circle that sent a Shadow scurrying away.

Paul gave a wicked grin as the Scythe returned to his outstretched hand. "And I got yours." Wes gave him a thumbs up.

"Keep your eyes on the prize, gentlemen!" Shayne's voice could be heard through the communicators.

"Our eyes never left the prize, Shayne," Paul said to her as he turned and swished his Scythe around hitting shapeshifting Shadows and causing them to run away from the Arions they were attempting to ambush. "If you think you can do better, you are more than welcome to bring those Jimmy Choo's out here and show us how."

There was no response from Shayne, but there were many smirks seen on the battlefield. Tia was twirling her whip around her head creating strong gusts of winds that were keeping the Shadows from being able to get to her; the winds sent them flying.

"How do we get to the prize when we take down one Shadow and two more takes its place?" Tia asked.

Her frustration could be heard as a Shadow managed to get by her wind-making whip and slam her on the ground. She swung her arm at the Shadow, and it went flying through the air.

"Even with our powers, they are making the goal difficult," she lamented.

"Difficult or not, if that giant wakes up none of us will survive her wrath," Kayne's worried voice came through the communicators.

Telara's Rotary became a shield to protect her from a general who towered over her and had brought a club down towards her.

"We need to work together and get to Darrold," Telara yelled.

She fell back as a Shadow Shapeshifter slithered behind her and whipped its tail out, wrapping around her legs and pulling her down.

"Oommph!" She knew she would have a bruise from that, something that she probably wouldn't have if she had been wearing her suit. However, she refused to say those words out loud, refused to give the Alaskans any reason to call her a Cheechako.

"Telly!"

I.Q. pulled back on the string of his bow to aim at the snake who was pulling Telara quickly behind it as it slithered towards a shadow cast by the mountain, but a Shadow minion slammed into him knocking him down. I.Q. brought his bow down on the Shadow's head causing it to let out a wail and back off.

"Telly!"

He rolled over trying to aim and let an arrow fly, but it just hit a nearby tree.

"Good thing Vanna isn't here," Chad muttered as he leapt into the air and brought his ice sword down on the tail wrapped around Telara's legs. They both looked down as the creature gave a shriek and slithered quickly away. The appendage that was still wrapped around Telara's legs started to wither and then became black smoke that dissipated into the air.

Chad helped her up, and his brother joined them. "If Vanna was here, it would even up the odds," he complained, his flail twirling in his hands.

"Well, she isn't, so we need to get through these Shadows to get to Darrold before she wakes the giant. Then we can go save our Mother Nature," Telara replied.

Telara started forward, her eyes on Darrold as she leapt over some minions that were heading her way. Turning her Rotary formed a whip which she used to hit each one in the back of the kneecaps. They fell to the ground screaming. Without Vanna here, they risked losing possible friends and allies, but it couldn't be helped. Turning back, she looked at Darrold whose mouth was moving. She didn't know what Darrold was saying, but she was sure it wasn't her mom's favorite recipe.

"Feeling inadequate yet, little Shadow fodder?" the woman in the cloak said to Telara, which had Telara jumping a bit and turning, but the woman was still a far way off standing on the boulder. Yet, her eyes were on Telara who was sure she was speaking directly to her.

"Of course I am," the woman spoke again, and this time it truly put Telara on edge. How did she hear Telara's thoughts? Telara hadn't even projected them to her friends.

"I could tell you." The woman offered and held out her pale porcelain hand. "I could tell you all you need to know, just come to me and take my hand. I will tell you everything that Lucius has not."

Those words stopped Telara in her tracks as she turned to look at the woman who had just basically offered Telara everything she had ever wanted since learning they were the Guardians.

Telara, stop! She is messing with your head, Cole's voice projected into her head stopping her movement as she realized she was actually walking towards the woman.

You can't trust her; she is just trying to distract you. She could hear the strain in I.Q.'s voice as he spoke while letting electric arrows fly.

"Are you truly so ready to walk away from the chance to learn everything they are trying to keep from you? Are you that pathetic?"

"She has nothing to tell us; she knows nothing," Tia said from beside Telara with her whip glowing brightly as it twirled around her creating so much wind that her feet were mere inches off the ground.

"Are you so sure?" The woman's smile was a combination of patronizing and malice. Telara shook her head. The smile turned victorious until Telara spoke loudly and with conviction.

"No, we aren't completely sure." She felt Tia twitch beside her. "But it doesn't matter. Whatever you have to tell us won't distract us from saving everyone. All you are is a distraction." She really wanted to know what the woman wanted to tell her, but she couldn't chance letting the giant wake up on the off chance that the woman would even tell them anything worth knowing.

"You are a fool then; you just gave up the truth to save those who use you as nothing more than fodder. If you think they care for you then you are not even worth my time you silly girl."

During this whole time, the woman's posture and expression had been calm and serene but now her eyes went from dull blue to a startling white while her face became pinched with her anger.

"Very well, you foolish child. You will lose here and with that loss you will be as ignorant as always."

It had taken Vanna several minutes to calm Nikos down. It was several minutes she wasn't sure she had, but she needed to find out who brought her here and why. She didn't like leaving her friends right before a battle; she never would have done such a thing. If she knew how to control that plant bud, she would have it take her to her friends.

"Okay, Nikos. Now who brought me here?" Vanna tried talking to the parrot who was staring at her while cocking his head one way and then the other. "Come on, Nikos! My friends need me!"

Nikos took to the sky and flew around Vanna then over to a tree that stood all by itself in front of Darrold's house. He flew around the tree but never landed on the branches.

"Squawk! I am a platinum member; I want decorations for my tree! Squawk!"

"Nikos," Vanna groaned kicking one of the loose stones that made up Darrold's driveway. "I don't care about any of your ridiculous demands!" When he flew over to the wooden railing and landed next to her still squawking about decorations for his tree, she turned on him with a frown. "Nikos, forget you-" Her words caught in her throat as something glinted in his feathers. "Nikos, what is this?"

"Squawk! Decorate my tree. I am a platinum member. Decorate my tree! Squawk!"

His wings spread out and flapped, but he stayed

there on his perch. Vanna reached out and there, nestled within the feathers around his neck, was a necklace. She gently lifted the necklace from the suddenly very pliant Nikos who just looked at her. Looking at the tiny silver pendant hanging from the silver chain, she saw that it was a leaf! A very familiar leaf. She looked at the tree in front of Darrold's home then back at Nikos who just stared at her.

"Decorate your tree?" she asked.

"Squawk! I am a platinum member! Squawk!"

Nikos took to the air and flew around the tree still squawking.

Vanna laughed. "Okay, okay."

She walked over to the tree, reached up, and hooked the necklace around a limb before stepping back.

"Your tree is decorated, Nikos. Now what?"

"Squawk! Wake up call for the platinum member! Squawk!"

"What are you talking about, Nikos?" Vanna watched as he flew over to the house. "Nikos, enough of this! My friends need me! I can't stand here and play games with you!" she hollered then turned around as a bright light blinded her!

Chapter 17

"Get away from me!"

Telara brought down her shield on the head of the Shadow that was attempting to stop her from getting to Darrold. Being a minion, it fell easily but then one of the bear shapeshifter ones took its place, reaching out for her with its paws. Before it could touch her, it let out a wail as Cole's fiery nunchucks slapped at its paws, chasing it away.

They stood there breathing heavily and staring at the chaos between the Arions and Shadows at the base of the mountain. The cloaked woman was directing the Shadows who followed her commands without any pause. As they turned to look at Darrold, they sighed.

"I know they could be friends and comrades," Chance said trying to catch his breath.

"But if we keep handling them with kid gloves, we aren't going to be able to get to Darrold," Telara finished for him. "Okay, kid gloves off. We don't have Vanna here, and we need to get to Darrold now!"

"Then let's get to Darrold," I.Q. replied.

I.Q. raised his bow, pulled back on the electric string, and shot out three light arrows that cleared several of the Shadows that were heading their way.

"Darrold! Stop!"

They started to climb the mountain to get closer to

Darrold who was still chanting in that eerie voice, her eyes still in that trance-like state.

"Don't hurt her!" Nat shouted at them right as a big bear-shaped Shadow grabbed her from behind. The Shadow threw back its head as its mouth opened in a painful scream. The Shadow let go of Nat, running away as Paul stood there with his Scythe in hand. Nat turned around and shouted to them.

"Just get her down from there."

Then she ran to help Paul out when several shape-shifting Shadows slithered from beneath a rock towards him.

"Great! Stop her but don't hurt her," Cole grumbled as they turned back to the mountain and started to climb the wooded rocky terrain. "Nothing t-"

The mountain rumbled from beneath them interrupting whatever it was Cole was about to say.

"What's going on?" Tia looked at them as they stood there frozen. "Tell me that isn't what I think it is."

"It isn't what you think it is," Cole said, but there was no humor in his voice or in his eyes. There was another rumble as they saw the stones beneath them move. They looked up at each other in fear and shock.

"The Sleeping Lady wakes!" the cloaked woman laughed and shouted in her maniacal voice.

"I really hate that woman," Tia snarled as the mountain started to rise beneath them. "Hope this giant steps on her."

"You and me both," Telara agreed.

Telara grabbed at a nearby tree as the mountain moved again.

"We need to get off this mountain before the giant completely rises."

They started to run towards the base of the mountain, leaping off the mountain as the giant moved and rose from her resting place. They landed hard on the rocky base.

"Look up!" Chance pointed up, and they saw Darrold losing her pixie form and changing back to the elderly woman they had first met. She started falling to the ground. Chance ran towards her, but he was too far away.

"He isn't going to get to her in time!" Telara placed her hand over her mouth feeling like she was watching a train wreck that she couldn't tear her eyes from. As they watched Darrold's fall, a wave from the water around the island rose and swept under Darrold. It gently carried her to Chance. The shock they felt lasted mere moments before they raced to where Chance was cradling an unconscious Darrold.

"How did you do that?" Chad stared at his brother in awe.

Chance looked up and shrugged. "I don't know, just glad I was able to." They nodded looking down at the unconscious pixie princess. "So, what do we do with her?"

"Can your waves take her back to Sanctuary?" Cameron walked up to them.

"I don't know, but I'm not willing to risk someone's life on it." Chance's voice was firm; it brooked no argument.

A loud wail that had everyone holding their ears interrupted them.

"Nekatla!"

Susitna was awake and demanding her lover.

The butterflies that were floating around in their stomachs became swarms of locusts at the sight of the towering giant.

"We need to get her to safety," Cameron spoke up looking down at the unconscious Darrold. Everyone nodded in agreement.

"I got her." Wes leaned down, lifting her into his arms. "You guys concentrate on making sure that giant doesn't get off this island. I will see if Kayne has any idea on how to get the giant back to sleep."

"No problem," was Chad's sarcastic reply, but Wes had already walked through the transporter with Darrold.

With Darrold now out of the way, they could concentrate on the giant who was looking around for her love and calling his name.

"Any ideas?" I.Q. asked as he held his bow at the ready, ready for what they didn't know.

A scream pulled their attention from the giant back to the battlefield where the Shadows were still attacking the Arions as they fought to push them back. Cameron shook his head and said,

"No clue, but I need to get back into the battle." He gave them an apologetic look. "Think you guys can handle the giant?"

The correct answer was no way possible but instead Telara nodded. "We'll keep her here while you guys take care of the Shadows."

"Good luck," he said before running back into the battle with his polearm swinging and taking out Shadows as he ran by.

"Are you nuts?" Cole asked her. "How are we going to keep her on this island? She is a fricken giant!"

"I don't know, but we're going to have to find a way," Telara sighed in frustration staring at the giant.

"Maybe we can reason with her," Tia suggested.

"Can always try it." Telara moved forward trying to figure out how to get the giant's attention.

"Nekatla!" Susitna hollered out again looking around for her love. Her voice so heartbroken that all of them felt a tugging at their heartstrings.

"Susitna!" Telara shouted trying to get her attention. When that didn't work, she started waving her arms around while jumping and shouting but still the giant cried out for her lover drowning out Telara.

"Susitna!"

They jerked around as the cloaked woman spoke, her voice amplified to be heard.

"This isn't going to be good."

Chad's words echoed all of their thoughts as they stood there frozen. The cloaked woman rose above the rock to speak to Susitna.

I.Q. pulled out his bow and aimed for the cloaked woman who was floating in air almost at Susitna's level. He let several arrows fly, but they never hit their mark as Shadows in the shape of birds intercepted them with painful screams.

"Not at all," I.Q. replied.

The woman turned her attention to them. Her smile was one of pure malice. They knew whatever happened next, they weren't going to like it.

"Your Nekatla can't come for you because of them." Her long black nails pointed at the Guardians. "If you want your Nekatla, you need to kill them."

"Nope, not good," Chance said as he backed away

then leaped out of the way as Susitna reached down to swat at them as if they were bugs. To her, they probably were.

The others followed his lead just barely missing getting knocked back. Instead, the air from her movement sent them sliding across the rocky ground. The rocks cut into them as they slid across them, and they knew they would be having some new bruises. Standing, they looked up at the very angry giant.

"She is lying to you, Susitna!"

Tia attempted to reason with her but had to jump as a fist landed right where she had stood. Rocks and dirt went flying hitting them all.

"You need to listen to us!" she tried again brushing the dust and rocks from her face. This time, she jumped out of the way of Susitna's large hand as it swept her way, landing on a gust of wind that held her up in midair.

"You're riding the wind!" Cole said in awe, something in normal circumstances they would have celebrated, but this wasn't normal circumstances. Under normal circumstances, they didn't have a giant trying to squash them.

"I'll keep her distracted and try to reason with her. You guys try to take out that irritating woman before she really riles up Susitna." They nodded as Tia used the winds to rise up so that she was in Susitna's face. "Susitna, you need to listen to me." She moved quickly as Susitna attempted to knock her out of the sky. "Stop it, Susitna! You're being tricked!"

Telara and the others raced to where the woman was standing on air while laughing at Tia's attempts to reason with Susitna. Seeing them running towards her, she turned. Her lips curled into a smile as Shadows appeared in their way.

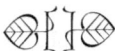

"Hello," a very pleasant voice said from the brightness. When Vanna could see once again, she was staring at a regal looking woman who stood where the tree once was. Her auburn hair fell down in waves, and her emerald green eyes were watching Vanna with curiosity and tenderness.

Vanna swallowed, looking from the spot where the tree had once stood moments before to where the woman was in a white looking toga dress with golden ties.

"Were you stuck in the tree or were you the tree?"

The female laughed, holding out her hand which Vanna took.

"My name is Mica, and I would like to thank you for freeing me from my earthly prison."

"How did you get put in there?" Vanna asked her then realized she hadn't introduced herself. "My name is Savanna, but my friends call me Van or Vanna."

"I would love to answer any questions you have but was I accurate in hearing that you have some friends who are in danger?"

Vanna slapped her head with her hand. "Yes, they are trying to stop the Shadows from waking The Sleeping Lady."

"Someone is trying to wake Susitna?" Mica's eyes widened as Vanna nodded her head. "Then we do not have any time; we have to stop that from happening."

"I agree, but I don't know where they are or how to get there." Vanna felt so helpless.

Mica smiled as the green bulb appeared from the ground in front of them. "Our chariot awaits."

"How will it know where it is going?" Vanna asked walking cautiously towards the bulb that had brought her here.

"It got you here didn't it?" Mica stepped into the center with a smile. "I promise you we will get there, and we will get there quickly."

Vanna stepped inside next to her and gasped as the leaves rose and surrounded them both pulling them back into the earth.

"We are of the earth, Savanna. It will do as we request as long as our intentions are pure."

Vanna nodded to her as she could feel the pod racing through the earth.

"Can you feel it?" Mica asked her and again Vanna nodded. "One day, you will be able to do this."

"I wish!" Vanna just looked around as the pod raced under mountains and water as it raced to The Sleeping Lady. "I couldn't imagine doing something this cool."

Mica laughed. "You need more confidence."

Vanna looked at her. "Will you teach me?"

"I would love to."

Mica smiled, and Vanna couldn't stop the smile that broke free. She had finally found someone who had powers just like hers, and she was actually going to teach her how to use them. She couldn't wait to tell the others.

"But first," Mica sighed. "We need to get Susitna back to sleep."

"She's awake?" Vanna felt her stomach drop. "Is Darrold okay? How will we get her back to sleep?"

Mica held up her hand just as the pod started to rise

out of the earth. "I only know what the earth tells me. Right now, it is crying out with Susitna's pain. As for how we will get her back to sleep, leave that to me." She smiled at Vanna as the pod opened up, and they both looked around at the battle taking place. "Go help your friends; I need to have a chat with a giant."

Chapter 18

Telara was flying backwards from being tossed by a Shadow creature that looked as if he could have been Susitna's little brother. She was heading towards some very jagged looking rocks near the shoreline.

"Telara!" Chad shouted as he tried to get to her before she hit the rocks. A nearby bush moved to catch Telara before she hit the rocks. They stood in shock before looking around and shouting out with glee.

"Vanna!"

Telara rolled over, joining the others running to Vanna and hugging her.

"Where were you?" Telara asked Vanna.

Vanna laughed. "I'll tell you all about it later but right now let's get these Shadows taken care of."

"Who is that?" Cole pointed up at Mica who was using the trees around the island to catch Tia who had gone flying from Susitna's well aimed slap. They ran to her as she fell to the ground dazed.

"That's Mica," Vanna told them looking down at Tia. "You okay?"

Tia gave a shake of her head and looked up at Mica who was standing on a very massive tree in front of Susitna. "I am now thanks to her."

"Mica said she will take care of Susitna," Vanna told them.

"That leaves the cloaked wonder for us." Telara grinned. "And with all of us, she won't stand a chance."

"Let's take her down!" Chance grinned as they felt a renewed burst of energy and hope with the appearance of Vanna, who truly made them feel like a team again. They started towards the woman who turned in their direction as they made their way to her.

"You really think you are a match for me?" she sneered as she raised her arm and pointed towards them. "Shadows! Don't let them pass."

Generals that were as tall as the trees around them lumbered towards them. They had minions that gathered around their feet with their dark claws extended. Tia started to swirl her whip causing massive gusts of winds that knocked the minions back, but the generals kept moving forward. Vanna placed her staff on the ground causing vines to grow up from the ground in an effort to stop the generals' forward movement.

"Time to warm these guys up!" Cole started twirling his nunchucks creating so much heat that Vanna's vines started to whither. However, before the generals could break free, Chance brought his flail down on the ground which brought gushers of water to burst up from the ground, spraying the generals and pushing them back. As they stumbled back, the shapeshifting Shadows advanced from the generals' feet in the forms of wolves and caribou.

I.Q. aimed his bow high and sent many arrows into the sky. They exploded above them and rained down electrical bolts that sent current after current through the Shapeshifters who screamed out. They cowered for a few moments before they shakily attempted to rise up.

"Stay down!" Chad shouted as he brought his sword down into the ground right in front of them. Ice formed from the sword and crept up on the shifters, minions, and generals, encasing them in ice.

Telara took off running. She leapt from the ground, landing on the back of one of the generals. She used it to launch herself up to the boulder where the very startled woman was attempting to flee. Telara grabbed her by her arm and, to Telara's shock, her Rotary started to glow brightly. The woman definitely wasn't a Shadow, so why the Rotary was reacting to her was a mystery.

"Get off me!" the woman snarled trying to pry Telara's fingers from her arm. However, it seemed the Rotary had other plans as the glow seemed to get brighter until it basically encased the woman completely. Telara could hear the gasps of the others, but she was unable to do anything but stare as her Rotary seemed to come alive all on its own.

Telara tried to release the woman but her fingers wouldn't let go, it felt as if they were frozen in place. Looking back, she could barely see the others who were doing their best to keep the Shadows from advancing on her as they stared up at her with worried expressions.

"Telara!"

She turned to see Gage running her way dodging Shadows. He did a half turn while whipping a crystal bomb at one that got too close to him sending it off screaming.

"Stay back!" she yelled still trying to pull her arm back, but Gage jumped over a shapeshifting Shadow that was attempting to stop him and landed on a smaller part of the big boulder they were on top of.

"Let go of her!" Gage hollered at her while trying to shield his eyes from the brightness.

"What do you think I'm doing? Dancing the mamba?" Telara shouted back in agitation as once again she tried yanking her arm free while looking anywhere but at the brightness in front of her.

The light had her so blinded that when she felt a touch on the arm that was stuck to the woman, she blanched. She turned, and there was Gage grabbing her arm trying to help free her.

"You idiot! You need to get out of here!" she shouted at him.

He shook his head as he gave another yank. "You don't leave friends behind!"

She opened her mouth to yell at him, but the light had grown in so much intensity that it felt as if it was burning her. She let out a pained yell that became strangled as an explosion sent both her and Gage flying several yards to land on the rocky earth.

Dazed and winded, she pushed herself up on her elbows and looked around. She saw the others sprawled in various positions on the ground along with the Shadow creatures that looked to be dazed as well. She looked up, but the woman was no longer standing on the boulder.

"Did you just defeat her?" Cole stared at her in complete disbelief.

"I don't know." Telara just shook her head then quickly looked to her side where Gage was holding his head looking around. "Gage, you okay?"

"If the ringing in my ears would stop, I would say yeah," he groaned giving his head a very wobbly shake.

She slapped him.

"Telara!" Vanna frowned at her.

"He should've stayed away when I told him to," Telara complained, upset with him for putting himself in danger and upset with herself for not being able to control the circumstances that caused him to try to help her out.

"You're welcome," Gage groaned as Cole came to help him up while Tia helped Telara off the ground.

The shaking of the ground reminded them of the giant Susitna. Turning around, they were astonished at what they saw. The woman that had come with Vanna was standing on the branch of a tree with her arms open. In front of her, the grass, plants, and trees were slowly growing back over Susitna who was laying back down just as peaceful as a babe laying down for her nap.

"There is no way she could do that so easily." I.Q. was staring in total disbelief, his scientific mind not understanding the logistics of what they were seeing. Only minutes before, the giant had been swatting at everyone and putting several of the Arions out of commission.

"Who is she?" Tia asked Vanna while the others looked on, curiosity brimming in their faces.

Vanna watched her. "She said her name is Mica, and that is all I got out of her. Oh, and she was a tree until I put a necklace that Nikos gave me on one of her branches."

"A tree?" Cole looked from them to the woman who was now being lowered very gently to the ground by the tree. "Cursed?" He looked back at Vanna who shrugged her shoulders.

The graceful brunette walked over to them in her white toga dress with a very gentle smile on her face.

"Hello."

She stopped in front of them clasping her hands in front of her. Cole and Chad practically tripped over each other to introduce themselves to her, so much so that they ended up on the ground at her feet. She knelt down.

"Are you two okay?"

They both looked up at her with an awestruck gaze. "We're just fine," they said together.

The woman laughed as Tia and Telara pulled them both off the ground while glaring at them. She looked over at Vanna.

"Hello again."

"How did you get the giant back to sleep?" Gage, who seemed to have finally gotten his bearings, asked.

Mica smiled at him. "She is of the earth, so I used the earth to lull her back to sleep where she will stay until it is truly her time to awaken."

"Hopefully, that isn't any time soon," Cole spoke, and Chad nodded in agreement.

Mica laughed. "No worries; it isn't."

"If you guys could pull yourselves away from your idle chit chat some help would be wonderful!"

At Cameron's voice, they spun around and saw that there was still some Shadows left standing who were attempting to make one last ditch effort in taking off with whoever they could grab.

Mica stepped forward with a smile. "Allow me."

Her voice so sweet but when she held out her hands, the flora all around them started to glow with her power. Power that, even as inexperienced as they were, they could feel was great.

Astronomical, Tia nodded speaking through their mind link.

Cosmic, Chance had to add as he watched the ground glowing beneath Mica's feet.

Mega, Cole practically sighed making them roll their eyes.

Herculean, Chad said as the glowing expanded out engulfing the Shadows that had been knocked out from Telara's burst of power.

Incalculable, I.Q. said watching the glow advance towards the Shadows fighting their friends.

Colossal, Telara even had to add as the glow overtook the Shadows that had been fighting their friends, what was left of them.

Vast, Vanna breathed, and they could hear the envy in her tone, not that they could blame her.

"I am not doing anything that you yourself are not capable of." Mica smiled at Vanna who looked at her with a surprised expression. "When you go to speak telepathically, you might want to make sure that no one can hear you; otherwise, it could come off as rude."

"Larry!"

They turned to see Paul, Dominic, and Jesse run towards a body that was unconscious on the ground. Gage sucked in his breath, and Telara was sure he was having flashbacks to when he was in that exact position.

"Get our healers here; we need evacs!"

Cameron started barking out orders, and everyone moved to get to their fallen comrades taken care of and ready for transport.

"There were a lot more Shadows than that," Tia said looking around at the unconscious bodies that were human, Arion, and mythicals alike. They nodded in agreement. While many of the Shadows had disappeared before Mica had done a mass healing on the land, there were still more than what they were seeing lying about.

They watched as the Arions worked to get all those that had been healed put on the stretchers that were being brought through the transporters. Cameron walked up to them.

"We have to get them back to the infirmary." He looked up at the mountain then at Mica. "Is she asleep for good now?"

Mica nodded. "Until it is her time to awaken."

Cameron seemed satisfied. Looking from Mica to Telara he said, "We need to get back to Sanctuary and get the injured taken care of."

Telara knew what he was telling them, that they needed to leave, but she wanted to ask Mica some questions and from the look on Vanna's face so did she.

Mica just smiled at Cameron. "I will make sure they get back safely."

Cameron looked at Telara who nodded. "We'll be fine, promise."

Cameron looked over at Mica before turning back to Telara. "I'll keep the com open if you need us." He glanced briefly towards Mica again who just stood there with a very serene smile on her face. "For anything."

Telara smiled at him gratefully nodding at him as he turned away and joined the others who were helping their wounded through the transporters.

Chapter 19

The Guardians stood alone on the island with the very beautiful Mica who had created herself a seat from the flora around them. It was not a throne as one might think but just a lounge seat full of green leaves woven together so perfectly that you couldn't see where one ended or the other began. Colorful flowers appeared as well around the lounge as if by design, and what a design they made. It was on that lounge seat that Mica now sat silently watching them. I.Q. kept giving the mountain nervous glances making sure to keep his distance. He wasn't the only one. Vanna was the first one to break the silence as she moved forward towards Mica.

"Mica, I would like to introduce you to my friends, the Guardians: Telara, Tia, Chad, Chance, I.Q., and Cole." She gestured to each of them as she said their names and they, in turn, gave a nod of recognition. It showed how awed they were by this new person that both Chad and Cole were speechless.

"Hey, Vanna! Can you make a chair like that?"

Well, for a brief moment they were. Telara pressed her lips together to hide her grin at Chad's question. Vanna just gave him a baleful look.

"No worries. You will, child," Mica told her still seated on her earthly chair.

"She will?" Both Chad and Cole said in unison

staring at Mica who just gave a nod. "Static!" Then they looked at each other before looking back at her. "What about us?"

Mica laughed, not a rude laugh but a purely gentle one as if their eagerness amused her. "You are all capable of great power," she told them. "It is up to you when you fully come into your own power."

"Then I'm ready now," Cole declared, puffing out his chest and holding out his arms. "I'm ready to Flame On!"

Chad was nodding vigorously in agreement while the others were shaking their heads.

"I don't think it works that way," I.Q. told them dryly while Tia laughed which pulled a disgruntled look from Cole.

Mica, though, just gave a soft little twinkling laugh. "You are right, I.Q.; it doesn't work that way. It takes a lot of practice and even more patience, but you will all get there."

"How do you know?" Telara asked.

If it were anyone else, Telara would just think they were handing out platitudes but for some reason, Telara felt that Mica knew what she was talking about, and she wanted to know why.

"Because you come from great power," Mica told them simply.

They turned and looked at each other in confusion. Vanna looked at Mica curiously.

"You know who our godly ancestors are?" Vanna asked.

"Don't say anything more, Mica."

They quickly turned around. There stood the male

they hadn't seen since they had released him from his imprisonment as a dragon.

"Hey, it's the dragon man!" Chad exclaimed which earned him a glare from Kull who was walking towards them.

Cole wasn't looking very impressed as he watched Kull come to stand by Mica on her lounge.

"Look who finally shows up," Cole said.

Kull looked at him, his eyes narrowing. "If you have something to say boy, say it."

Mica frowned at Kull then looked over at Cole. Her eyes widened before she turned watching Kull closely, her eyes narrowing as if she had just realized something.

"Where have you been?" Cole asked him, causing Kull's stance to become more guarded.

"I don't see where that is any business of yours, boy."

"Kull!" Mica's soft-spoken voice held censure, but neither Kull nor Cole were paying her any attention.

"Really? I seem to remember we were the ones who released you from your imprisonment as a dragon; yet, we haven't seen you since," Cole accused him, his face growing red in his anger. Telara and Tia were looking at each other not sure what was going on exactly. Even Chad looked stunned at the reaction from Cole who was usually joking and good natured. Even when dealing with Raven and her cronies, Cole never seemed to get this riled.

Kull was the only one who didn't seem affected by Cole's outburst. His manner and expression were that of a statue as he watched Cole. "Where I've been or where I'm going is no one's business but mine. I don't owe you anything but the thank you I already gave you for break-ing that curse."

"Not even an explanation?" Cole stared at him.

"I was cursed, and you broke it. Explanation over." Kull crossed his arms.

"You know more than you're saying," Cole said, his voice harsh.

"What I know is none of your business." Kull's manner was starting to get on all of their nerves; he was being purposely difficult.

"Fine! Keep your secrets but go away and let someone who might actually know something help us out." Cole crossed his arms basically mimicking Kull. "At least Mica is willing to be helpful to us."

I thought Telara was supposed to be the antagonistic one in the group.

Telara looked over at Chance, her face showing her disbelief, not because he would say that, but that he would say that NOW. Chance just shrugged as they turned back to the drama happening in front of them.

"Mica isn't going to tell you anything; it isn't her place to do so."

"Kull, you don't speak for me." This time, Mica's voice held no sweetness as she stared at Kull, her aggravation plain in her expression.

"Just 'cause you don't have the guts to tell the truth doesn't mean no one else does," Cole told him. You could hear the intake of breath all around as Kull's expression darkened.

"Kull!"

Mica rose and started forward. Her intent had been to walk between them; instead, a wall of fire blocked her.

"Kull!" she shouted at him.

"Stay out of this, Mica," Kull said to her, but he never turned away from Cole who was refusing to back down.

"This boy is my concern, not yours."

"I'm not your anything!" Cole spat back at the man, his fists clenching.

Cole, you might want to tamp down that hostility.

They nodded at Tia's words which were full of worry, but Cole acted as if he didn't hear them.

"You should heed your friend's warning," Kull told him sending a wave of shock through them all.

He had heard them?

Cole didn't even acknowledge his words and what they meant. Instead, he fired back, "I'm not scared of you."

The fire wall expanded so that it encircled both of them, blocking off all of the others from getting to either one.

"Brave words, but that is all they are: words."

"Kull, they are just learning," Mica said to him, but he just shrugged.

"Then let's consider this class in session," Kull said as he lowered his arms to his side. "Never make a challenge you can't back up unless you plan to be just another of the Shadowmaster's puppets."

"Oh, so now you know all about the Shadowmaster?" Cole sneered. "Funny, the last time we spoke, you didn't know anything about him or the Magine."

Kull shrugged as the wall started to close in around them both. When the others moved forward because they were worried about their friend, Mica shook her head at them with a very disappointed look on her face.

"He is our friend," Tia protested as the wind started to kick up.

"Wind and fire don't mix around plants and trees;

you might want to take that into consideration before you create a disaster you won't be able to control." Kull's voice held contempt. He never took his eyes off of Cole who was staring right back at him. If looks could kill, Kull would surely be six feet under.

"Leave Tia alone! She knows how to control her power!" Cole shouted at him.

Telara looked at Tia whose eyes looked strangely glassy.

"Hmmmm…" Kull looked between Tia and Cole thoughtfully.

"Kull, NO!" Mica's voice raised in warning, but it was too late. The wall of fire that had once surrounded Kull and Cole receded quickly into the ground only to rise around Tia, separating her from the others who were knocked back by the flames.

They stared in horror at the wall of flames that started to close around Tia who had created a wall of wind around her to keep the flames from getting too close. Unfortunately, it seemed to be backfiring as the flames started to ride on her wind, making her wall of wind become another wall of flames.

"Tia!" They jumped up to try to save her, but each one of them found themselves blocked by fire. Telara turned to glare at Kull.

"Stop this, or we will stop you!" she shouted, but he just shrugged looking unaffected by what he was doing.

"Only Boy Wonder here can stop this." Kull shrugged ignoring their angry glares and Mica's very reproving looks.

The walls of fire started to burn brighter heating up the very air around them until they were sure they would come out of this either very tanned or looking like lobsters. Cole looked from Tia to Kull, his expression one of pure hatred.

"You have something against me, you take it out on me. Leave Tia alone!" he shouted. They watched the air around him crackle as flames kissed the air.

Kull's expression never once changed. "You're running out of time, boy. You can keep shouting and throwing a temper tantrum over something you can't control, or you can do something about it. What will it be?"

Cole glared at him, but a frightened scream from Tia had him jerking around. He ran to the wall around her, reached out towards the flame, and shrunk back as his hands came in contact with the flames. He looked back at Kull breathing heavily.

"Stop this! I'm sorry alright!"

He let out a growl of frustration when Kull said nothing but kept watching him. Turning around, he stared at the wall of fire. He closed his eyes and breathed in deeply before letting it out. Everyone was watching and sending prayers to whoever was listening as Cole stood there with his eyes closed breathing in and out.

"Whatever you are going to do, Cole, do it soon," Telara whispered as softly as she could, her stomach fluttering once again with those dang locusts as she watched the scene in front of them play out. Every time they attempted to move forward, the fire in front of them would move as well blocking any rescue attempt. If this showed Telara anything, it was they really needed to learn more about their powers.

Vanna gasped and Mica's worried look eased as they watched the air around Cole start to heat up as he pulled the flames from around Tia so that they swirled around him instead. They watched all the flames that blocked them start to dissipate as the flames were pulled into the already growing ball that surrounded Cole.

"Flame on!" Chad breathed, and Telara saw what he was talking about. Cole looked like a human torch standing there, exactly like the one in that movie the guys all loved watching.

Cole turned to look at Kull who was watching him, his expression still impassive. Telara was sure the hard look in his eyes changed but to what she couldn't describe. Cole raised one arm with his palm facing Kull, and they watched as all the flames that had become part of Cole's body become a ball of flame that shot out and slammed into Kull.

They stared in shock as Kull was tossed back several feet into a boulder. The ball of flame exploded around him, creating a black silhouette in the boulder around his body.

Mica turned to give an approving smile to Cole who had already turned away from Kull. He had extinguished the flames that had surrounded his body and was helping Tia to stand. Tia was staring at him as if seeing him for the first time.

"You okay?" he asked her, and she gave a dazed nod while he wore a triumphant grin.

"Dude, did you see what you did?" Chad had broken from his amazement to run over to where Cole and Tia were. "You flamed on! First, Telara takes out the Shadow lady and then you flame on!" Chad sounded astounded and excited all in the same breath. His head jerked from one to another so quickly, they were surprised that he didn't make himself dizzy.

"So, what do you have to say for yourself, Kull?" Mica's voice took on a lofty note as she smiled proudly at them.

They turned and saw Kull rise from the ground, brushing the dirt and soot from his clothes. His clothes looked more modern than when they had first met him. How they missed that they didn't know. He was wearing a black T-shirt, jeans, and black boots.

"What I have to say is that it is time that we left," was his autocratic reply.

Telara just stared. She could feel the emotions coming from the others, and they were a mirror to hers: astonishment, confusion, and a touch of irritation that Kull couldn't even acknowledge what Cole had done.

"It doesn't matter," Cole said, still standing by Tia who was leaning heavily on him as she attempted to get her bearings back. "He doesn't have anything we need."

Kull snorted. "I just helped you grow your powers, boy. You would think you would be more appreciative."

Before any of them could reply to his arrogance, Mica reprimanded him. "If you are calling that teaching then you need a lesson in common courtesy."

"They have a destiny in front of them that they aren't even close to being ready for." Kull shrugged. "They need to grow up and fast; that won't happen with mollycoddling." He gave Mica a pointed look which, from the glower on her face, wasn't setting well with her. A rumbling was their only warning as the ground beneath Kull's feet shot up, catapulting him far into the air and away from the island.

Mica turned to them with a smile and dusted her hands. "Kull is right; who needs mollycoddling?"

They laughed at her words, but their laughter faded as she sighed.

"I better leave; he will just come back and be more of a jerk."

"But we need some answers! You can give us some guidance," Vanna protested.

Mica walked to Vanna, lifting her hand to cradle Vanna's cheek. "I won't be far but for now maybe it is best if you learn some things on your own. I promise, when you need me, I will be there." She looked over at Cole. "And so will hothead."

She smiled and stepped back as a plant appeared, lifting her up. She waved to them as the petals closed around her before the plant disappeared into the ground.

"Will we ever get any answers?" Telara sighed.

"We did get some answers," Chance said looking at the spot where Mica had disappeared. "Or at least a glimpse of what Vanna is capable of."

"Great," Chad grunted. "Just what we need: Savage capable of tossing anyone several thousand miles who irritates her."

"Hey!" Vanna exclaimed frowning at him for using the nickname given to her by some of their classmates during gym when she had pelted one of Raven's cronies with the dodge ball after they caused a new girl to run away crying. Vanna might be the gentlest of them all but when it came to defending her friends or anyone who was being bullied or repressed, she could turn savage; hence, the nickname. "Careful or you'll be the first victim when I'm able to do that."

Chad gave a nervous combination of a chuckle and giggle, which caused everyone to laugh before Tia radioed Cameron that they were ready to come back.

They were walking towards the transporter when Telara saw a movement out of the corner of her eye. Turning around, she saw a dark-haired man in a trench coat watching them. She blanched when the male nodded towards her as if in greeting before disappearing from sight.

"Let's go, Telly," Tia hollered at her.

After one more glance at the spot where the male had stood only seconds before, Telara hurried after her friends. She didn't know who that was or why he was there and to be honest, she was done with riddles for a while.

Chapter 20

They were back at Sanctuary under the water watching as a tall lanky Larry was sitting on one of the beds in the infirmary cracking jokes with Wes, Dominic, and Paul. Watching them, you wouldn't think that Larry had been gone for over a year spending his life as a Shadow slave to the Shadowmaster. His leg swung back and forth as he grinned at his buddies. His brown hair curled around his ears and nape of his neck.

Jesse and Glen were standing there laughing and looking pleased as well as many others in the infirmary. Unfortunately, they also stood around others who didn't look as alert as Larry.

"Jesse has to be happy to have Larry back," Gage said as he and Zeke joined them.

"Why is that?" Vanna looked from them to the joking and joshing group.

"Larry was…is," Gage corrected himself, "Jesse's second."

"Glen won't like that." Cole looked over at Glen who was grinning at Larry. "Although he is hiding it pretty good."

Zeke laughed. "He isn't hiding anything; Glen never wanted to be second. Being second in the Delta Faction means more work than being a leader in all the other Factions."

"Why is that?" Chance asked.

"Well, at least here in Alaska," Gage said watching them. "In Alaska, they are the most called upon Faction and when they go out tracking, they could be gone for weeks at a time. And in doing so, they encounter more of the mythicals in Alaska which means they need to know all the different rules and practices for each race."

"Not something I would want." Zeke nodded.

"But you are a Delta leader," Tia informed him.

"But we aren't in Alaska and in the states, we are able to see everywhere with our view screens." Zeke shrugged.

"And we also don't have different magical tribes," Gage added. "Remember, all the mythicals are in Sanctuary."

"Not all." Zeke grinned but before they could ask what he meant by that Kayne approached them.

"Kaleth and Juneth would like your company."

He spoke so formally they looked at each other wondering what they did wrong; Darrold was returned safe and sound.

"What did we do now?" Cole said their thoughts out loud and not one of them reprimanded him as they looked at Kayne waiting for his answer. However, before he could answer them, Gage gave a sound of complete shock, his eyes and mouth wide as he stared straight ahead.

Turning, they felt the same surprise although they were certain that Gage's had to feel more like a fist to the gut. Larry was holding a glowing rope in his hand that he was now doing tricks with; the kind that rodeo cowboys do. It wasn't just any glowing rope; that was his Crim and he was working it.

They turned back to Gage to say something, but their words stuck in their throats. What could they say? They didn't know why Larry was able to use his Crim after what happened when Gage was denied that ability.

Gage just shook his head. "Let's go see what the King and Queen want."

"They only asked for the Guardians," Kayne told him gently, but Vanna interrupted him.

"If they want to speak with us then they can speak to Gage and Zeke as well." Her words brooked no argument; even when Gage went to speak up, he went silent with just one look from her. Their savage could silence a banshee with just a look if she wanted.

"This way," Kayne spoke, and they followed.

"I don't recall asking for the other two," Kaleth haughtily said as they entered the conference room followed by Gage and Zeke.

Vanna walked past everyone and took a seat at the head of the table, her head held high. "Either they stay, or we leave." She stared at the King without flinching.

Are we going to end up beheaded?

No one grinned nor acknowledged Chad's very legitimate question as the King and Vanna continued their stare down.

"Enough of this," came the lofty voice of Queen Juneth as she placed her regal hand on her husband's arm. "Our daughter is waiting for us back home. Let us get this manner taken care of so we can take our leave."

King Kaleth reluctantly pulled his hard stare from Vanna giving his wife and Queen a look of tenderness.

The look disappeared as he turned to them gesturing for them to take a seat at the table. They noticed that Kayne had not left the room as he took a seat next to Gage. Gage was sitting next to Vanna who had the air of someone who wasn't in the presence of a king and queen waiting for a judgment to be handed down.

"We would like to thank you for your help in rescuing our daughter."

They stared at him not sure they had heard him right when Kayne spoke up.

"This rescue was a group effort Your Majesty, not just the Guardians."

Kaleth looked at him with that regal look. "You and your warriors are allowed to stay here on our land, that is your payment and always has been. These humans aren't from this establishment, and I refuse to be in debt to any humans." He turned back to them. "So, what shall it be?"

They stared at each at a loss for words. This wasn't really what they were expecting.

"So, what shall it be?" Kaleth asked them again looking regal as he stood before them seated at the table.

They looked at each other in confusion. In one sentence, he says he wants to reward them for saving his daughter but in the next makes them feel as if they were no more than a slug he had just stepped on and needed scraped from his boot.

"What if we refuse?" I.Q. crossed his arms and leaned back in his chair. Everyone turned to see what the King had to say.

"Why would you refuse?" The king had a perplexed look on his face.

Vanna gave a very unladylike sound, and they held their breath. When she got riled up, anything could come out of her mouth.

Or flying at you.

Cole reminded them of the time Vanna got so upset back home during art class when the antagonistic carrot top Chet decided to pick on one of his favorite targets: one of the silver-haired flower power twins, Starla. He didn't like them because they were different. They believed the stars spoke to them in different ways. A nearby bowl of green paint had turned Chet's red hair green, not to mention the wall and cabinets he was standing next to, when Vanna had tossed it right at him. They had ended up staying after class and helping her clean up the mess. Starla, the flower power twin Chet had picked on, had stayed and helped as well.

They were brought back from their memories when Vanna spoke.

"Why would you want to reward someone who you seem to look down on as if we aren't even good enough to be breathing the same air as you?" Vanna stared at both the King and Queen, not flinching once.

"You misunderstand me," the King attempted to say but at a look from Vanna, he sighed. "No, there is no love lost between my kind and you humans that pretend to have our best interests at heart." When Vanna opened her mouth to protest, he held up his hand with his autocratic manner. "You asked," he pointed out and by the pinched look around Vanna's tightly pressed lips, she didn't appreciate him pointing that out.

King Kaleth held out a seat to his Queen. It was only after she had seated herself that he took his seat and continued.

"The Sanctuary that you all hail from is used to the mythicals around you living under your rule."

"We don't rule them!" Zeke protested standing up with his hands on the table. One raised brow from the king had him slowly sitting back down with a mumbled, "Well, we don't."

"So, they are free to come and go as they choose?" Kaleth asked.

"They have their own town where they have lives, jobs, and even relationships," Zeke argued.

"That wasn't my question." Each word was spoken very distinctly, letting Zeke know that Kaleth wanted an answer.

Zeke's lips pressed together so tightly they almost disappeared completely. It was Gage who spoke next.

"Life in the lower 48 is much different than here in Alaska. If they were to be seen by any human outside of Sanctuary, it could cause problems."

"So, they are not free to come and go as they choose?" Kaleth asked again. This time, he looked at Gage.

"No," Gage said taking a deep breath. "But neither do we treat them as inferiors."

"Ahhh, so they are allowed to work alongside you in this Sanctuary?" Kaleth said, and Telara flinched when he stressed the word allowed. He made it sound like an insult although she was pretty sure it was an insult to him.

"They have jobs at Sanctuary," Gage told him tightly.

Telara and the other Guardians looked at each other but said nothing. It was only recently that the mythicals now worked at Sanctuary. After the battle at Sanctuary when the Shadows had invaded and the mythicals fought alongside them to defeat the Shadows, it had finally been acknowledged that they were able to defend themselves and were able to procure positions in Sanctuary. But they weren't going to be the ones to point that out.

"Menial jobs or do they actually work alongside the warriors of Sanctuary?"

Gage acquired a tick in his jaw at Kaleth's words, and they worried that this situation was going to end up barring them out of Alaska just like Claw.

"They aren't able to work the Crims to battle the Shadows," Gage said pointedly.

"Are you?" Kaleth asked. The whole room sucked in a breath at that.

Gage's face went white at that question, and his voice sounded very restricted. "No."

"Yet, you fight alongside your friends with weapons that were fashioned for you to use against the Shadows."

While Zeke and Gage both looked highly uncomfortable with the line of questioning, neither the King nor the Queen looked perturbed one bit.

"I am not attempting to make you uncomfortable or start a battle of words."

A snort from Zeke had Kaleth shaking his head.

"I am just trying to explain our aversion to being in debt to you. Your mythicals live under your rule; they don't police themselves or take care of their own disturbances. They depend on you to do so which puts them under your care and under your rule."

"That was what the magical community and Sanctuary agreed upon for their own best interests," Gage explained.

"When the decision of one takes away the freedom

of another, it is never in their best interest," Kaleth told them.

"It wasn't just the decision of one," Zeke protested. "We would never do such a thing. It was the council of mythicals and our leaders that made the decision. Together." Zeke made sure to put an emphasis on the word together.

"It was decided by a few who claimed they spoke for the many," Kaleth told them. "Now, they live by human rules; we don't and never will."

"So, exactly what is it you are offering us?" Telara asked before the all-out war they felt brewing in the room actually happened. She had a feeling no matter what Claw had done to get banned from Alaska attacking a royal had to be worse.

Kaleth looked at her. "Name it and if it is within our power then we will grant it."

Telara looked over at the very pale Gage. She felt bad for him when Kaleth pointed out that he couldn't work the Crims. He had been so nice to them when they first came to Sanctuary when Pam had been giving them such a hard time. She wondered… Looking around at the others, they nodded with a grin. She turned back to the King.

"Can you give Gage back his ability to work the Crims?" she asked. She could hear Gage choke on air at her words, but she kept her gaze on the King.

King Kaleth sighed. "Alas, the first thing you ask is something that isn't in my control. We can't grant him a power that we have never had."

Telara slumped down in her seat; she had really hoped that they could help Gage.

Why not ask if they have answers about the Paladins or the upcoming war with the Magine, I.Q. suggested and, for a moment, they thought about that. They weren't sure if the King would have the answers they needed, but wasn't it worth a shot?

Or we could ask if he could grant Claw a stay of execution. They looked over at Cole with similar looks of confusion. You know, get his ban from Alaska revoked.

They looked at each other, momentarily weighing the options: to get Claw's ban lifted or get answers they not only wanted but needed to live.

The information he gives us might not help us, Vanna gently spoke up. Telara knew she was right but just the thought of them possibly being able to get some answers was very tempting.

"If you can't think of something, I can have some of my pixies bring some treasures from our land for you," King Kaleth suggested, his manner showing that he was getting anxious to leave them.

One last look at everyone and their decision was unanimous. She turned to Kaleth.

"Can you get Claw's ban lifted?" she asked and heard the surprised gasps from both Gage and Zeke.

"Is that what you want?" Kaleth asked them, and they nodded at him. "Very well, consider it done." He rose from the table. "And now with that done we have a daughter to attend to." He gave a regal bow and turned away to take his Queen's arm. "Thank you for your help and please don't take offense, but I do hope our paths never cross again."

With those words, he and his Queen shrunk down in size and flew off.

"Don't take offense? How don't you take offense to something like that?" Chance looked around indignantly.

"You learn not to," Kayne grinned as they rose and headed out of the conference room.

"Will he really lift the ban on Claw?" Vanna asked Kayne.

Kayne nodded. "The mythicals around here are nothing if not true to their word and if he couldn't do it, he would definitely have let you know. I'm sure we will have word before end of day that Claw's ban has been lifted, and I know one king who won't be happy about that." He gave a chuckle that had them feeling as if that fact didn't bother him any.

Chapter 21

My whole stash of fizzy buzz juice?" Larry stared at his friends as if he couldn't believe what they were telling him.

"Man, you were gone for a long time." Dominic shrugged before taking another big bite of pizza.

"I was captured by the Shadows!" Larry exclaimed.

"Yeah, what was up with that?" Wes shook his head at him. "You let those spineless, no heart, no soul creatures get the better of you? Man, thought you were better than that." Wes lifted his mug to his mouth hiding the grin that was there.

"You snooze you lose." Paul leaned back in his chair with a big grin while Larry just stared speechless at them as if he couldn't believe what they were saying.

"Alright guys, that's enough."

Jayne and Lisa walked out shaking their heads and putting a big case down in front of Larry whose face went from disbelief to pure excitement.

"My fizzy buzz juice!" he exclaimed opening the case and taking out unlabeled bottles filled with orange looking juice. Telara looked at Tia and Vanna who were sitting there with her watching the show while waiting for the guys to join them. They both gave the bottles distrustful looks.

"How about your girlfriend?" Lisa looked at him

with her hands on her hips. She was very pretty with brown hair that fell around her face in ringlets. They weren't close enough to see the color of her eyes, but she had a very pretty smile when she had first walked out with Jayne. Now, she was frowning at her boyfriend who was looking from her to the jars of fizzy buzz juice. When she went to turn around Larry jumped up and wrapped his arms around her grinning at her.

"You know you are the most important part of me." There was that smile they saw earlier. "You brought me my fizzy buzz juice!"

Lisa was smaller than Larry but with one quick swipe of her feet, Larry was sitting on the floor. The sound of his heavy thud echoed all around the cafeteria. Lisa walked away from him while he shouted behind her.

"Just kidding baby!"

"Not a dull moment here at Sanctuary."

They turned and saw the dark-haired lanky Gamma leader grinning at them.

"If you think Lisa has a temper, you should see when Wes gets Jayne going." He motioned to the other girl who had walked out with Lisa, the one standing right next to Wes with her hand on his shoulder. She looked as if she had to be the smallest Arion here. "Don't let her size fool ya; she has been known to send Wes flying over a table a time or two."

"That girl?" Telara pointed right to Jayne to make sure they were talking about the same girl. She would be lucky to even reach Wes's shoulders when he stood up. Jayne was standing there watching Larry run after Lisa. When he caught up to her, Larry lifted her up in his arms and swung her around. Jayne lifted a hand to tuck a stray brownish blond strand of hair behind her ear.

"Haven't you learned anything from watching Paul, Wes, and Dominic practice? When it comes to skill, size doesn't mean anything, and Jayne is one of our best fighters." Cecil grinned as he also watched Lisa and Larry.

"Where were they during the fighting?" Tia asked. Telara had wondered the same thing. She was sure they hadn't seen either of them nor did she know when they had gotten back, and Larry was recovering.

"They are two of our best fighters and two of our best negotiators," Cecil shrugged.

"Negotiators?" Vanna frowned. "What do you need negotiators for?"

"To keep all the tribes from declaring Sanctuary a danger to all the mythicals here," was the very concise answer.

"How could they consider Sanctuary a danger?" Vanna frowned. "We saved the princess."

"They might be thinking without Sanctuary being here there would also be no Shadows," Tia pointed out, and Telara could see how the tribes could think that.

"But that is just silly," Vanna protested. "The Shadows created Sanctuary not the other way around."

"You have to remember, there is no one still alive that can confirm or deny that," Patches said as she approached them. She was wearing her ever present jangling tool belt, leather work boots, a turquoise flannel shirt, and shorts. "So, the tribal rulers have been petitioning their elders on the council to revoke our status here."

"What would happen then?" Vanna asked.

"Sanctuary would become property of the mermaid

tribes as this is their domain, and we would all be transferred to different Sanctuaries," Cecil said simply.

"And then they would have no protection from the Shadows," Telara said shaking her head. "Don't they see that?"

"They believe without Sanctuary here the Shadows will disappear." Patches shrugged, and Cecil gave a solemn nod.

"Right now, the elders have been able to keep our status safe, which is why we always have to be cautious in how we handle things," Cecil told them.

A snort had them turning to see Chance standing behind them. They didn't know how long he had been listening, but it must have been for several minutes at least. Cole and Chad were moving closer as well.

"I say let them deal with the Shadows if they think they can do without Sanctuary," Chance said.

Cecil shook his head. "That wouldn't do anything except get us banned quickly. All we can do is what we have been doing."

"Well, that blows," Cole said harshly, but Cecil and Patches both had the same look on their faces: the look that said that that was something they were used to.

"We need to get everyone rounded up and head back home before we do something to get ourselves banned from Alaska," Zeke half joked as both he and Gage walked up to them. Gage looked to be rather solemn. Since the talk with the king and the remark about him not being able to use the Crims anymore, he seemed morose.

"I heard you got Claw's ban revoked?" Cecil looked at them with a grin.

Telara shrugged. "They offered us a reward, and that is what we asked for."

"Pretty unselfish reward." Patches looked at them with a look that resembled admiration. They started to squirm at that look, not at all comfortable with it. They could handle the confrontational looks but not this.

"Yeah, well, like Zeke said, we need to be heading home," Telara said, starting to move away.

"Tell Claw I can't wait to see him." Patches gave a smile that resembled Fritz's smile back home. It was a smile they weren't sure they trusted, so they just nodded to her before turning away to find I.Q. so they could get out of there and head home.

Telara stopped as a thought occurred to her. Turning back to Cecil, she said, "What is fizzy buzz juice?"

Cecil laughed, but it was Patches that answered. "It's a concoction of Larry's but don't ask us what's in it."

They looked at each other for a moment before nodding and walking away.

"You guys really did it!"

They had just rounded the corner almost to the Command Center where they would be saying their final goodbyes when they ran into Drake and Jess.

"Did what?" Cole asked with a guarded expression they all knew so well; they had seen it many times after being confronted by a teacher who had their lesson plan exchanged with the coach's play sheet or a principal who ended up with a black circle around his mouth after using a bullhorn at an assembly.

"You lifted Claw's ban!" Drake grinned at them. "Big

time, man!" His excitement had them grinning.

Telara gave a lift of her shoulder. "They said they would grant us anything we wanted and since they couldn't grant Gage his powers back, we asked about lifting Claw's ban."

"Seems saving a princess trumps cursing a prince," Jess snickered.

They had a feeling there was more to that story but before they could ask Jess held out her hand to them. They just stared at her hand, their curiosity growing.

"I won't bite I promise," she giggled. "I just wanted to shake the hands of the ones who got the arrogant Fae King's edict overruled."

There has to be a story here. Chad looked at them, and they gave a silent nod to his telepathic words.

But no one seems that inclined to share it, and we do have to head home, I.Q., the voice of reason, said.

They gave silent agreement as they shook Jess's hands. Telara turned and smiled at Drake.

"It was great meeting you and seeing Alaska, but I think it's time we went home now." She held out her hand, and Drake shook it.

"You guys go," I.Q. told them as they turned to leave. "I want to ask Drake something."

"Don't miss your transport home, dude," Cole told him with a smirk. "Might not be another for, oh, another minute or so." The others just shook their heads at him, and Jess pushed him forward.

"Come on, Andrew Dice Clay. Let's get you out of here before your poor jokes get you buried in the sound floor."

Jess gave him a not so gentle push every time he would

stop. It seemed she was ready for Cole to go home, something they were all in agreement about.

When the others were gone, I.Q. turned to Drake.

"That book you have, why haven't you ever shown it to Claw if you guys think so highly of him? I would think that book would be something he would kill for."

Drake gave him a funny look. "Why would I show Claw?"

I.Q. blinked, taking a step back. "A book that has to do with crystals, and you don't think Claw would be interested?"

Drake's funny look turned to one of complete astonishment. "How do you know that book is about crystals?"

"I don't know that the book is about crystals for sure but before the battle at the merkingdom, I saw a passage saying something about crystals having hearts or something like that." I.Q. put his hands in his pockets, doing his best to not show his curiosity.

"Big Time!"

I.Q. jumped back at Drake's shout. He gave him a very cautious look as Drake looked like he was about ready to cut right into dance and song.

"Sorry, man! But this is the first time anyone has ever been able to read anything from that book." Drake's eyes were bright with excitement.

"Really?" I.Q. blinked a few times at the rapid shaking of Drake's head. "Then why do you even have it if no one can read it?" I.Q. scratched his temple.

"That book was passed down from Arion to Arion here in Alaska with the same instructions," Drake told him and pulled out the very ancient-looking book, from where I.Q. wasn't sure, but there it was in his hands. "To give it to the one that could decipher the text. It has been here waiting for you, man. Big time!" Drake's big time echoed down the hallway around them.

"I.Q., we're going to leave without you, man! Hurry up!" Chad shouted out from the Command Center down the hall.

"You better go, man," Drake clapped his shoulder. "I would love to hear more translations from the book if you would."

I.Q. nodded. "Big time."

Drake let out a hearty laugh, this time giving I.Q. a clap that almost knocked him over. Drake grabbed his shoulder to steady him and laughed. "Now you're getting it. But one word of advice: I would be careful of who you tell about that book." I.Q. gave an understanding nod; he had a feeling this book was very valuable indeed and not in a monetary way.

"Thanks, man."

I.Q. turned and jogged down the corridor.

Chapter 22

They had said their goodbyes and promised Kayne that they would make sure to give Lucius the message to contact him. Standing on the transporter, they watched the view before them change from the Alaskan Command Center to the Sanctuary they were used to, along with Claw who was watching them with narrowed eyes.

"What did we do now?" Cole asked as they stepped down from the transporter.

"I dinna do well wi being in anyone's debt," Claw told Cole as he looked at them with a scowl. His accent was thick in his irritation.

"Deal with it," Vanna told him as she walked by him giving her head a toss and leaving the others standing there staring and feeling a bit dumbfounded.

"What was that about?" Claw frowned at them.

I.Q. gave a confused chuckle and shrugged. "No idea."

"So, news travels fast," Chance said stepping down and grinning at Claw who was still frowning at them. "It wasn't that long since we requested that your ban be lifted."

"The minute Cecil heard he was on the vid screen tae me." Claw shrugged then gave one of his roguish grins. "Wish I could be thare tae see the good ole Fae King's face when he found out. Pixies trump Fae!" He let out a bark of laughter and turned to walk away.

"Claw!" Telara called out to him, stopping him just as he was about to walk into his office. "What did you do to get banished from Alaska? Since we got it lifted, you could at least tell us that."

Claw paused a moment as if contemplating whether he wanted to tell them. It was driving them crazy trying to figure out what he had done.

"Let's just say I gave the prince an attitude adjustment."

Telara just glared at him. That wasn't an answer and by the twinkling in his eyes, he knew it.

"Last time I saw the Fae prince, he had gills."

Telara's forehead crinkled; the others' images mirrored hers as they tried to figure out what he meant. Tia gasped looking at Claw with wonder. Claw's grin grew bigger.

"Adrijan? You did that?"

"Adrijan? The crazy mermaid?" Chance looked from Claw to the others who were all looking astonished. "You turned the Fae prince into that crazy mermaid? How?"

Claw's grin was a cross between "jokerish" and psychotic as he went into his office and shut the door.

Cole looked at them, his expression reminiscent of a child being told that Christmas was being canceled. "He can't just say that and walk away."

"He did," Tia told him point blank.

"He has to tell us how he did that."

Chad nodded in agreement to Cole's protest.

"You two are the last two that need to know how he did that," Telara told them while shaking her head at them.

"That I agree with." Gage stepped down bumping

into a nearby table of newly created Crims in their re-laxed state. One would have hit the ground if he hadn't grabbed it quickly. They stared in astonishment as the Crim glowed brightly in his hand, but none looked more shocked than Gage himself.

"Big time!" Cole hollered out. The others just groaned at that before clapping Gage on the back congratulating him.

"Don't know how that happened but couldn't have happened to a better dude." Zeke grinned.

"You guys do realize that when you get back from missions there is such a thing as filling out the reports, right?" Pam said up from the door, her amused look turning to one of wonderment when she saw the Crim shining brightly in Gage's hand. She looked at him. "See if it will transform for you."

Gage lifted the Crim in his hand, and they watched as it glowed brightly before transforming to a black metal pole with a serrated blade at the end. The crystal was black as well as the pole, but it still glowed.

"A Japanese Naginata sword!" Chad breathed out, his eyes wide. He shrugged feeling their eyes on him. "I know my swords."

"How?" Pam looked at them, but everyone just shrugged their shoulders. They were just as confused.

"Does it matter?" Cole clasped Gage on his shoulder. "The man is back!"

Gage snorted. "The man never left." But they could all see how much more alive he looked standing there holding that very bright sword.

"Well, fine then; the power is back." Cole huffed. "Now time to eat."

"Why am I not surprised," Tia laughed as they walked out of the Gamma's quarters and headed down the hall.

"Hey, guys."

They turned to see Pam staring at them.

"Mission means reports. If you think I'm doing them for you then you have all lost your minds."

"Come on, Oh Mighty Alpha leader," Chad grinned at her. "Gage has his mojo back; we should celebrate that. Czar's Cantina! Drinks on me! Celebrate now, reports later."

All the tables had been moved so that they could sit together, even the mythicals joined listening to them tell the stories about their adventures in Alaska. They kept out the shapeshifting Shadows for now; they wanted to talk to Lucius first. They laughed at the story of Nan and Bobby, well everyone but the gnomes who frowned gasping when they said how Nan threatened to cut off his beard.

The story of Cole getting caught in a shed by a moose got the whole place laughing, even Cole laughed at it after a moment or two. They were sitting there drinking Silest's punch and munching on fries as they listened to Serdita play her Chenras. They looked at each other thinking about Soliel and her violin Chenra, something they had left out of their story. They weren't even sure about whether they should tell Lucius everything she had said, or even anything she had said. If he wanted to keep them in the dark maybe it was their turn to do the same.

The only problem with that is that he knows more than we do, I.Q.'s voice of reason said silently in their minds.

Stella walked in, her brown hair swaying behind her in her ponytail. She sat down next to her leader. Pam raised her hand for Daphne to bring another glass. Taking the glass, Stella looked like she was about to explode with information.

"Spill it," Donny told his Faction mate, his green eyes sparkling.

"More Shadows got healed."

Everyone stared at her announcement.

"You mean the ones that couldn't be healed?" Vanna's eyes widened as she leaned forward.

Stella nodded. "Most of them, but enough to sway the leaders to not agree to Ira's plan."

The table erupted in cheers and glasses being raised in toasts. Vanna's smile was the biggest and brightest of them all.

"So, what did you think of Alaska's Sanctuary?" Pam asked them, trying to not look as curious as she truly felt. Telara grinned. For someone who had started out as one of their biggest adversaries, Pam had become one of their best allies, and she felt as if she was starting to understand Pam a bit more.

"It was so static!" Chad grinned.

"Don't you mean Big time?" Cole said, his eyes sparkling as he spread his arms out and linked his hands behind his head.

It amazed them how everyone in the cantina all shook their heads, some groaning, some rolling their eyes, and then there were the amused chuckles.

"I take it Drake's Big time is well-known?" Telara looked over at Pam who just nodded.

"He had Gabe saying it for weeks when he returned

from there," Brie said with her fingers held up not looking at Gabe who was sitting next to Vanna while frowning at Brie.

"Do we even want to talk about your experience?" he asked her with a raised brow.

"What did you think of the merpeople's kingdom? The first time I saw it from their Command Center it looked so majestic," Brie asked them not even acknowledging what Gabe said as she pushed a red lock of hair behind her ear.

They looked at each other, not sure they wanted to talk about what had happened at the kingdom considering the merpeople's reaction to it.

"Still looked majestic," Vanna, ever the diplomat when she was inclined, responded.

"Looked?" Gabe turned from giving Brie pointed glares for ignoring his comment to staring at Vanna with a curious look.

"Well, there was a battle there," I.Q. said slowly staring into his punch. "It got banged up a bit, but we helped repair as much as we could."

Telara knew he was still sore over them not being able to question the merpeople regarding what their buildings were made of. To tell the truth, she was as well.

"Oh?" Stella asked looking very interested.

"Yeah." Chad nodded his eyes going big. "Fighting the Shadows under water, that was an experience. Of course, it probably wasn't a big deal for Chance," he grumbled elbowing his brother.

"Just because I'm a good swimmer who can control the water doesn't mean that it wasn't a big deal for me," his brother protested. "First time I've ever fought under water for any reason."

"I wasn't aware that Shadows could swim," Tobias, the brown-haired Omega leader, said from the wall behind them. His voice startled them as they hadn't seen him enter the cantina.

"Trust me, they can," Tia snorted.

"Especially when they grow fins," Chad grimaced. So much for not talking about the shapeshifting Shadows, but the reactions of everyone around them had them curious.

"Fins!" Donny's eyes grew wide.

"Yep, and then you have the ones with tentacles," Cole, not to be outdone by Chad, had to point out.

"The battle was intense for sure," Vanna agreed.

"Forget the battle; I want to hear about the Shadows with fins and tentacles!" Donny exclaimed.

"Forget the battle? The battle was intense though," Chance argued.

"We have never heard of Shadows with fins or tentacles," Donny spoke up.

Looking around, they saw they had the attention of the whole cantina.

"How about Shadows that slithered or looked like bears?" Tia asked which had everyone's attention. She looked over at the other Guardians who were realizing this news was completely new to all the Arions around them, which shouldn't be a shocker considering the Alaskan Arions were shocked as well.

Think Lucius will know of these Shadows?

All of the Guardians shared the same look of uncertainty at Tia's question.

Guess we will find out tomorrow, Telara answered while looking away from the table to where Serdita was playing.

She turned back to the table where everyone was talking about the Shadows that resembled the Alaskan animals. While the Arions were barraging the other Guardians about the different types of Shadows, she moved away from the table and walked over to where Serdita was sitting with her Chenras moving along her hand making beautiful music.

Serdita looked up at her and smiled. "Hello, Guardian of the Mind." Her voice was just as melodious as the Chenras she played, but they had gone silent and still in the palm of her hand.

"Guardian of the Mind?" Telara frowned at her.

"You are a Guardian, and your power is the power of the mind, am I not right?" was her simple response. Telara was seeing the resemblance between her and Soleil at this moment.

She nodded. "I am, and I guess that means you're right."

A delicate brow rose. "You guess?"

"Uh…" Telara was taken aback for a moment. "Okay…you're right."

Serdita smiled. "Of course I am." She lifted her hand, and the Chenras started playing again.

"We met your sister," Telara quickly said, expecting more of a reaction than Serdita smiling with mild curiosity.

"Which one?"

Telara stood there with a stunned look on her face. "What do you mean which one?"

"Which sister of mine did you meet?" Serdita didn't stop playing her Chenras as she asked the question very slowly and deliberately.

"There are more?" Telara asked feeling dumbfounded. She was sure she had been told that Serdita only had one sister.

"Yes." Such a simple word spoken; yet, such a frustrating word. Serdita was no more informative than anyone else that should be guiding them along this frustrating time.

"How many more?" Telara asked her.

"How many more sisters?" Serdita asked as the Chenras moved along her hand. "Or brothers?"

Telara blanched. "You have brothers as well?"

Serdita watched the silver balls moving. "You act as if that is shocking to you. You don't think I am able to have brothers as well as sisters?"

"I didn't mean that," Telara hastened to say instantly regretting her reaction. She worried she had offended Serdita, but Serdita just gave a twinkling laugh.

"No worries, Guardian of the Mind; I am not offended. I have three sisters and four brothers."

"Seven siblings?" Telara asked her.

"Yes." Serdita nodded. "Seven." Serdita looked up at her, and Telara blanched as she looked into her eyes. She swore in those eyes she saw visions of Serdita, Soliel, and some others together. One looked like the male singer from their favorite group they had seen last year with Pam. Sezen was the singer's name.

"Hey, Telly!" Cole's voice carried across the very noisy cantina. With the interruption, the images cleared to the green of Serdita's eyes.

"It seems your friends have noticed your absence."

Serdita turned away, concentrating once again on her Chenras as if stating the conversation was over. Telara nodded but knew it was far from over, not while she was still a Guardian. If Soliel knew things, then she was sure Serdita did as well. However, for now, she would let it be. She nodded to Serdita before heading back to the table. Cole was describing the big battle at The Sleeping Lady. Telara snorted to herself; he was exaggerating per usual. Of course, it didn't take Tia long to correct him.

And that is how the fight started.

This was going to be a long night, she sighed as she sat down.

Chapter 23

Telara woke up the next morning back in her room at the bungalow, her squiggly friends playing around on her ceiling. She couldn't contain the disappointment she felt; she had slept through the night with no visit from Zach. Turning over in her bed, she pulled the blanket up to her neck and sighed. She didn't understand why he didn't come see her, but she knew she already missed him. She heard her friends moving around in the bungalow and knew it was only a matter of time before they came to wake her up. With a groan, she rolled out of bed; they had a debriefing to go to.

❈❂❈

Growing up as a normie, as Claw called anyone who lived outside of Sanctuary and knew nothing of their world, debriefings were similar to what one saw on crime shows where everyone sat around a table drinking coffee with folders full of papers in front of them. At Sanctuary, it meant sitting around a glass table with gnomes running around grumbling as they placed cups on the table along with carafes of water. Telara was seated next to Pam who had Gage on her other side. Claw was standing behind them leaning against the wall along with Cole, Chad, and Chance. Tia sat on the other side of Telara with I.Q. and Vanna, who were waiting for the preliminaries to get over with so they could fill everyone in on what they had experienced.

At the other end of the table, Lucius sat with Ira at his side and the other heads of the Factions as well. Carmen sat next to Ira with not a hair out of place in her tailored clothes and giving them looks of disdain, as if sitting there with the other peasants was beneath her. Zeke was on the other side of Lucius with Tobias, their voices low as their heads practically touched while they conversed and ignored everyone in the room. Gabe was between Tobias and Vanna leaning back in his chair and looking around the room with a hooded gaze.

Ira had to clear his throat several times before Zeke and Tobias would look up from their conversation. He leveled a hard stare at them, but they just grinned. They could sense Claw grinning from behind them; anything that irritated Ira made Claw happy. Ira's disapproving gaze moved from Zeke and Tobias to Telara and the other Guardians. Telara stared back at him refusing to squirm or let him know how uncomfortable that look made her.

"We have been informed of how you saved the pixie princess and that the monarchy offered you any reward that you wanted."

"Then I'm sure you were told what it was." Cole linked his hands behind his head looking sideways at Claw who didn't even acknowledge him, although the look of irritation on Ira's face seemed to make Claw's lips twitch into a semblance of a smile.

"What I want to know is why," Ira didn't ask; he demanded from them. "I find it rather odd that you would be given an opportunity to ask for anything you wanted from one of the most powerful monarchs in Alaskan mythicals; yet, you waste it on lifting a banishment."

"Waste?" Vanna straightened up glaring at Ira. Telara, Tia, I.Q., Chance, Chad, and Cole knew Vanna was about to go savage, and that was never a good thing.

"Dinnae waste yer temper on him, lass," Claw drawled not moving from his position. "He's not worth it." Vanna still glared at Ira, but she just pursed her lips and sat back, saying nothing else.

Ira's face showed his displeasure, although they weren't sure whether it was because he didn't get a rise out of them or that Claw said he wasn't worth it.

"And how do you explain Gage's sudden return of his ability to use the crystals?"

"Miracle?" Vanna suggested her voice still irritated as she stared down Ira, daring him to argue with her.

"Does it bother you?" Telara asked him. She wasn't understanding this debriefing at all. She was expecting questions about the Shadows and the woman they saw, not this.

Ira turned his gaze to her. It became a very unamused one as he responded. "Why would you say that?"

"Why ask?" This came from Pam, and Telara was sure she saw a slight surprise in Ira's eyes when she asked. Telara looked over at Gage, but he sat there saying nothing.

"Aren't you even curious as to how this 'miracle' even happened?"

"Sure we are," Tia spoke up. "But more than that we are just happy for Gage, aren't you?"

"Let's move past what we know happened and move on to what we don't know," Lucius broke into the conversation when it looked as if Ira was about to respond. Lucius looked at Telara. "We were told you had some Shadow problems while you were there."

"Problems?" Telara huffed. "That's what you call Shadows showing up and kidnapping a pixie princess, attacking the merpeople kingdom, and trying to wake a giant that has been asleep since only the Gods know when?"

"Yes, I do believe that is what we call Shadow problems," Lucius told her in that calm voice of his, but in his ice-blue eyes there was a twinkle.

Before Telara could retort, Tia started to tell all about the battles with the Shadows in Alaska including about how the Shadows took the shapes of the animals around them except for during the battle at the kingdom of the merpeople where they became squids and other aquatic animals. Lucius listened to her, his eyes showing no reaction except when she told about the Shadows actually shifting their shape during the battle at The Sleeping Lady and when she spoke of the reaction from Telara's Rotary that had knocked them all out. His eyes widened just slightly. If Telara hadn't been watching him for a reaction, she wouldn't have even noticed it.

Ira looked accusingly at Telara. "Your Crim reacted to this woman who controlled the Shadows? Why did it do that?"

Telara's eyes narrowed momentarily as she felt an angry burn at the accusation. "Gee, we've only known about being Guardians and this world for a year while you guys have known about it all your life! But be my guest and demand answers from me!"

"That was uncalled for!" Ira sputtered his face turning red.

"No, your accusation was uncalled for," Pam told him shocking many in the room as she looked at Ira and refused to look away. "They have been asking for answers that no one wants to give them since coming here. They are putting their lives on the line with no explanation as to why, except that it has always been that way. They are here asking for answers again, and your words along with your manner were more of an accusation than an attempt at understanding. You may not have meant it to be that way, but that is how it came off."

Ira stared at Pam, and they could sense the internal struggle within him. Pam rarely stood up to him but since Telara and they had come to Sanctuary she had started questioning him outright. She tried to keep it as respectful as she could but sometimes, like now, one could hear the irritation in her voice at his manner. He wasn't used to this and from the side glare he shot towards Telara, they were sure he blamed her for this outburst.

"You're right, Captain," He said very tightly, each word sounding as if it had been forced between his lips to be spoken. "Accept my apologies, Guardian. I am sure you understand my frustration with hearing about these happenings with no actual explanation for them."

Seriously? He basically orders you to accept his apology and then thinks he is frustrated with not knowing what is going on? As if his life is on the line?

None of them contradicted Cole's outrage. After all, he was only speaking out their thoughts even if it was only to each other via their mind link. Telara was half tempted to speak his words out loud, but Lucius speaking up stopped her, which was probably a good thing.

"Besides shapeshifting Shadows and your Rotary's

power amplifying is there anything else we should know?" he asked them. Thanks to Ira distracting her, Telara had forgotten all about Lucius' little reaction to the news. His expression was once again the serene, calm face they had come to know. It was that which had her opening her mouth and saying something she hadn't planned on saying.

"Depends on whether you think Serdita's sister playing her violin and telling us that we are being lied to is newsworthy." Telara crossed her arms watching Lucius, but he gave away nothing.

"Did she tell you about what you were being lied to?" he asked. She wasn't sure if the interest in his manner was true or if he was just pretending for the sake of the others.

"About who we are," she told him.

"And who did she say you were?" he asked, his demeanor the same.

"More than just Guardians," I.Q. told him. Telara could hear the suspicion in his voice.

"Is that so?" Lucius leaned back in his chair watching them.

"I think a talk with Serdita is in order," Ira blustered standing up. "We deserve some answers."

Lucius stood up. "You are right, Ira, but first I need to speak with the leaders and let them know of these new developments. They will decide whether or not we confront Serdita and what actions will be taken." He turned to leave the room.

"Will they be able to tell us what Soliel was trying to tell us?" Telara asked him, stopping him as he reached the doorway.

It was almost a full minute before he spoke. It was so long that Telara thought he was just going to ignore her and walk out.

"I don't know, Telara, but I will be sure to ask."

This time, he turned and looked at her with eyes that were brimming with emotion; what emotion it was she wasn't sure, but she could see it there. She trusted him. Even after all they had heard in Alaska, she trusted him. She wasn't sure if it was a foolish thing, but she did.

She nodded at him showing her support, and there in his eyes she saw another surge of emotion. He turned quickly and left the room.

Do you think he will find out anything? Tia looked at Telara doing her best to not show they were chatting privately as others in the room started to rise and leave.

I don't know. Telara felt a lump rise in her throat but quickly swallowed it.

Do you think he will tell us if he does? Chad asked the question that Telara was trying to avoid thinking about.

I don't know. This time, it was harder to swallow that lump but as Pam turned to them, she tried to paste on a smile she wasn't feeling.

"We will find some answers one way or another," Pam promised them. They just nodded. "Why didn't you say anything about Soliel last night at the cantina?"

Vanna shrugged. "We aren't even really sure exactly what she said. It isn't like being told we are being lied to is shocking honestly. We just don't know who is lying or why."

The look on Pam's face showed that she understood their frustration. And while Telara knew she understood, it still didn't help their situation; however, neither would snapping at a friend who has only been trying to help them.

"Let's worry about that later; we still have time to decipher the riddles. The Magine isn't awake yet, and this time we WILL go into the battle more informed. Our fate won't be the fate of other Guardians. We have something they didn't have." She grinned at Pam. "We have friends." As she said the words, she knew they were true.

Cole put his arm around Claw who just looked over at the offending limb with a raised brow. "Yes, we do!"

Claw looked back at him. "You want to start wearing orthopedic shirts?"

Cole quickly moved his arm, and the others laughed.

"Come on, guys! Let's get in some training while we wait to hear what the leaders have to say."

Pam laughed as they filed out of the room groaning at her words.

Chapter 24

Lucius stood in front of the cupboard in which the statues of the dragons resided. There were two dragons: one white dragon holding a crystal ball that told of each coming of the Guardians and one black dragon holding a crystal ball that told of the awakening of the Magine. The awakening of the Magine that always meant the Guardians would go to fight her and never return.

How he wanted this time to be different, these Guardians who were different from their predecessors. These Guardians were the ones he had been waiting for. He knew it deep in his bones but now…

Before he lost the courage, he pulled open the doors, his heart clenching in his chest as he stared at the dragons. The white one stood there with the ball still glowing white, but the black one was still silent. He stared unable to believe his eyes.

"Were you wanting me, Lucius?" came the melodious voice of Serdita from behind him.

Lucius turned around leaving the doors of the cupboard open with both dragons sitting there and looking at Serdita with a look of betrayal, but Serdita showed no reaction as she stood waiting for him to respond.

"Has she risen?" he asked her, his voice tight with emotion. If Telara had been there, she wouldn't think he was the calm irritating voice of reason that she was used to seeing. Neither his voice nor his expression showed any of the calm the Guardians were used to seeing.

"Yes," Serdita responded.

"How?" he demanded then pointed to the silent black dragon. "It still sleeps. You told me-"

"I told you the truth," Serdita cut him off, walking along his office, her petite hand gliding along the shelves, books, and pictures that lined the walls as she moved further into the room.

"The truth?"

How often had Lucius heard Telara respond to him in the same way he was responding to Serdita right now? Too many times.

"You told me that the Guardians would come into their power before the Magine awoke, that she wouldn't awaken until they were ready."

Serdita was looking down into the Power room of the Guardians, abandoned as the Guardians were in the Command Center earning new bruises from training with the Factions of Sanctuary. She turned to look at Lucius.

"This is something you have been trying to circumvent since the prophecy was born all those years ago." Her voice held no accusation, merely fact. Lucius didn't bother to argue. How could he when she was right?

"How could I not? Each cycle, I had to teach a new set of Guardians knowing that all I was doing was training them to die!" The pain in Lucius' voice would bring a normal person to tears, but Serdita did nothing. "You promised me that the cycle would end, that it wouldn't last forever."

Serdita nodded. "The first beat of the crystal heart

would be the trumpet to start the final battle and end the cycle of death."

"I haven't been able to find the crystal heart. I've been looking for it, but it isn't anywhere. I have asked you for help, but you answer me with riddles that don't have answers. Now she is awake, and we don't have the crystal heart." Lucius' voice so tight with emotion it was almost choking him. He almost missed the look that crossed Serdita's face.

"You haven't figured it out?" she asked him, giving a low little laugh. "The Magine woke up, and the dragon didn't once wake up? It can only be the beating of the crystal heart that woke her."

"But how? Where?" Lucius' asked her, his voice showing his emotional turmoil. "We can use it to help the Guardians. Hell, I could even join them in their battle against her with the crystal heart."

Serdita shook her head at him. "The heart has already chosen it's champion, and it isn't you." This time, her voice held compassion. "I know you want to right the wrong you believed you took part in, but this is no longer your fight. This is the Guardians' fight now; they are who she wants, and they are going to be the only ones to be able to defeat her."

"How can they defeat her without the heart?" Lucius demanded.

"For so long, the heart hid itself in a corner between metal posts that kept its power hidden from the darkness that coveted it. Until, that is, it connected with a kindred spirit as lost as the heart itself was. On that day, the heart beat once again and woke the Magine."

Lucius shook his head at her and was about to argue

with her some more when something she said turned on a switch of sorts. The metal posts.

"Telara's Rotary," he said with wonder staring at Serdita who just smiled and nodded. "Why didn't you tell me? You should have told me."

"Would it have made a difference?" she asked him and when he opened his mouth, she shook her head. "No, it wouldn't have. But now that you know, you should celebrate. The Guardians have the power they need; they just need to learn how to use it. See, Caretaker, not all is lost, not yet."

"If they have the power they need, then I should be able to tell them all that I know, so they understand what they are truly up against." Lucius started to feel the weight that was always bearing down on him start to lift, until he looked at Serdita who was sadly shaking her head.

"I am afraid not; your promise still binds you."

"A promise I didn't want to make," Lucius spit out staring at her.

"It was a promise that was needed at the time," Serdita told him. "And it is still needed."

"The Guardians deserve to know what they are up against; they don't deserve to be kept in the dark."

"What about the Paladins, Caretaker?" Serdita asked him. "Are their lives worth giving the Guardians peace of mind? When the Guardians find out what you gave up for their peace of mind, do you think they would think it was worth the cost?"

"This isn't right," Lucius spoke between stiff lips, hating the fact that she was right and wanting to argue with her but knowing in the end that it wouldn't change anything.

"It never is, but it is the only way. The Guardians will need the Paladins for their final battle, this I have seen." Serdita gave him an understanding smile. "The path I told you of all those years ago is still possible; I still see it every night, and it is only getting stronger. The Guardians will win, and you will be reunited with him."

Lucius' head whipped up at her words, but she was already moving towards the door.

"So, your siblings are allowed to give the Guardians answers, but I cannot?"

Serdita stopped but didn't turn. "We are not bound by any promise. As seers and prophets, we speak to those that warrant our information. No Gods or any other divine creatures shall stop us from our paths. We do what must be done to ensure that the light will always shine."

With those words, she walked out of Lucius' office leaving the door open and Lucius standing by his desk staring at the dragon that was no more than a statue now.

"You shouldn't be so hard on them," Mica reprimanded Kull as her vines moved about the room putting a kettle on the stove and getting the teacups ready for them.

"They aren't toddlers to coddle, Mica. They are supposed to be warriors. If they want to play warrior then I will treat them like a warrior," Kull growled leaning against the wall in the kitchenette off of Lucius' office.

Mica didn't turn once, she kept her attention on the kettle that was starting to boil, but a vine moved along the floor and wrapped itself around Kull's legs jerking him to the ground. He jumped up and growled at her.

"Dammit, Mica! Quit using your dratted plants to do your battle just because you are wrong!" he roared.

"I never said I was wrong," Mica said lifting the kettle and pouring three cups of hot tea.

"You always use your plants or dirt when you're at a loss for words." Kull dusted himself off glaring at her.

Mica lifted a petit shoulder in a delicate shrug. "Maybe I consider using my plants on your hot head because it would be nicer than my words." She sat the cups down on the table.

"What do you find so funny?"

Mica turned around to see Kull glaring at Lucius who was standing in the doorway smiling at them.

"Oh, Kull, do go take a cold shower if you cannot be nice. Hello, Lucius! Just in time for some tea."

"Don't mind if I do," Lucius said as he sat down at the table lifting a cup up for a tentative sip.

Kull snorted, "Come here to side with her too?"

"Actually, I just came for the tea," Lucius told him and was met with a look of disbelief.

"Oh?" Mica asked as she sat down on a bushy chair that formed just for her. "Here I thought you might have come to tell us what Serdita had to say."

Lucius shook his head. "Always the observant one," he joked, but Mica just sipped at her tea waiting for his response. She wasn't one to demand answers, at least not verbally.

"Serdita? Wasn't she the one who told you to play patsy to the Gods?" Kull spoke, his face darkening. Lucius nodded.

"Yes, said it was the only way to protect all of you and finally defeat her," Lucius replied solemnly as he stared into the dark depths of his tea, dark as the Shadows that had taken so much from him.

If Lucius had been looking up, he would have seen the look of sympathy in Mica's eyes, seen her reach for him. Kull placed a hand on her shoulder giving her a hard look and shaking his head. She sighed, pulling her hand back. When Lucius looked up, she was smiling at him. She hated to admit it, but Kull was right; now was not the time.

"You did what you had to; we don't blame you," she said instead. At the scoff from Kull, a vine bonked him on the head causing him to let out some very colorful language that had Lucius grinning again.

"If smacking Kull is all it takes to make you smile, I will have to do it more often."

Kull gave her an incredulous look. "More often? Woman, I'm lucky I don't have brain damage as much as you beat on me."

"I don't think that is something you have to worry about," Mica said with a very satisfied smile as she took another sip. Kull's brow furrowed for a moment until what she meant sank in and then he glared at her.

"Real funny." His words were more of a growl than words.

"Your dragon is coming out again," Mica told him still sipping her tea with a very amused expression.

Kull just grumbled and sat down, picking up his tea and taking a big drink before coughing and wiping his mouth with the back of his hand. "Make this hot enough?"

Mica raised a brow at that. "Mr. Hothead can't handle the heat?"

Lucius let out a loud laugh interrupting Kull's disgruntled response.

"I have missed you both all these years," he admitted.

"I would say I have missed you as well but for me it was like I was sleeping all these years; time was like a dream for me. I could see the world changing around me, but it was more like dreaming. When my child woke me, I woke with knowledge of the time that passed but not how I ended up that way." Mica placed the cup on the saucer. "Do you know what happened?"

Kull snorted, "He knows but so far hasn't been willing to share very much."

Lucius sighed. "I fear that is no longer possible."

The look of surprise on Kull's face turned to one of anger as a voice spoke from behind them.

"Your promise, Caretaker!"

Chapter 25

Lucius sat there drinking the tea that Mica had made, his back to the doorway where the dark-haired God in his dark trench coat stood. He didn't turn around; he didn't need to.

"I wondered how long before you would show up."

"Hades!" Kull growled rising from his seat, his hands glowing red. Even Mica looked unhappy to see the God of the underworld standing there.

Hades didn't even acknowledge Mica or Kull; his dark gaze was fixated on Lucius who still hadn't turned around.

"You gave your word, Caretaker; you know the consequences of breaking it."

Lucius sat there with his elbows on the table and cup between his hands. "I know the consequences of breaking my word, Hades. But telling them the truth isn't breaking my word."

"How do you figure that?" Hades practically gritted out between his teeth.

This time, Lucius put down the cup and turned to look at Hades. "I made a promise that I would never reveal what I know to the Guardians; I never said I wouldn't tell the Paladins."

Hades' eyes grew wide. "Your play on words doesn't change what you promised."

"My, as you call it, play on words is fact." Lucius stood up to his full height looking at the God. "Your brother was so worried about the Guardians finding out the truth and calling him out on it that he never stopped to think that the Paladins, whose disappearances he himself orchestrated, could be freed." Hades eyes narrowed at him, but Lucius didn't back down. "The situation has changed."

"How so?" Hades didn't seem to believe him.

"She is awake," Lucius told Hades who scowled while Kull and Mica both looked confused.

"Your Guardians are already trained?" Hades frowned.

"No," Lucius told him.

"That isn't possible!" Hades looked perplexed at this news. "Your seer said she wouldn't awaken until the Guardians were ready," he said, his words spoken tightly. "You pulled us into this war of yours and now you can't even control the chaos that you caused," he said accusingly.

Kull stood up so quick his chair skidded across the floor and slammed into a nearby cupboard. "It was your brother and his wandering eye that pulled you into 'our' war."

"Actually, I think it had more to do with his hunger for power which allowed him to be deceived," Mica said softly, still sitting on her foliage throne and drinking her tea. She looked right at Hades before she spoke again, not wanting him to think that she was a wall flower. "At our expense, of course."

Hades' eyes widened at her words.

"Oh yes, being cursed didn't mean I wasn't awake,"

she informed him. "You hear a lot of things in the wind." She took another sip of her tea but chose not to elaborate; she wanted him to wonder. After what his family had done to hers, he deserved to wonder exactly how much she knew. She wasn't even looking at him, letting him know she was done with him.

"And if it wasn't for your brother, she would have died all those millenniums ago," Kull told him standing there with his fists clenched.

Lucius finally stood up, placing himself between Hades and Kull. He did not want this to turn into a war between the two. He didn't think the bungalow could withstand that. "We need to deal with the matter at hand. With her back, we all need to work as a team. It looks like the final battle is upon us, and we can't afford to lose this time."

"Do you even know where she is hiding?" Hades asked him with a dark look.

"Ask your brother," Kull sneered.

"He would never hide her." At Kull's disbelieving snort, he amended his statement very ungraciously. "Not again, that is."

"Excuse me if I have little faith in the word of a Greek God," Kull scoffed.

"You Greeks are why are our children have been sent to their deaths," Mica reminded him, still seated but no less dangerous.

"It was your seer who cursed your children to die," Hades snarled at her. Kull moved as if to attack the God who barely acknowledged him.

"Your brother threatened to kill them all!" Lucius' hand slammed on the table. "Her prophecy was the only way to not end their story forever. In her prophecy, they would awaken again and again." Lucius gave a defeated sigh. "To cover up his mistake, he would have let the world go up in flames. The children of the Paladins chose to follow the prophecy for someday it would bring back their parents."

"Our blood was sacrificed so that your secret never saw the light of day." Mica's voice was full of pain.

"And you don't think Zeus wouldn't still let the world die just to protect his secret?" Hades asked them with a cold look.

"I think your brother isn't as powerful as he used to be," was Kull's mocking retort. "If he was, he would have done something about us being free."

Hades snorted. "What do you mean by that?"

It was Mica who answered Hades. "The prophecy states that one day when the Gods' powers waned, the power of the Paladins would rise again and with that rise, the truth would be revealed."

Hades' face was redder than Cole's flames and with no more words, he vanished in black smoke.

Lucius sighed. "We really need to work together this time."

"We tried that the first time; I ended up as a dragon and Mica a tree," Kull grunted.

Mica stood up causing Kull to watch her warily. "On this, I happen to agree with Kull." Both Kull and Lucius had mirrored expressions of shock. "Because of those Gods and Goddesses, we have not only been cursed but separated from our loved ones." She looked at Lucius. "I don't trust them and until we are all back together, I would feel better if they stayed on their side of this realm."

With those words, she walked towards the doorway as her green throne slowly slithered back into the floorboards and down to the ground below. Just as she reached the doorway, she turned around.

"You still have some questions to answer, Caretaker. Don't think I have forgotten. If not for how exhausted I am from healing those poor creatures the Shadows infected, I would insist on them now. However, for now, my questions will wait. But not for long."

She turned around in her regal demeanor and walked out of the room.

"You know you won't be able to distract her like you do the others." Kull grinned at Lucius who just sighed.

"I know."

"I almost feel sorry for you." Kull gave a grin that had no humor in it at all. "Almost."

The cloaked figure walked up the rickety steps leading into the old decrepit house that looked as if one strong gust of wind would be the end of it. The landscape around the house looked as dead as the house; not one green blade of grass grew from the blackened dirt that looked as forbidding as the house itself. The trees resembled those one would see in horror movies with no leaves or sign of life, their bare blackened limbs reaching to drag a person to the depths of Hell itself.

None of this seemed to affect the cloaked figure as it moved through the doorway. The door barely clung to the frame; the hinges were so rusted you could no longer see the brass brilliance that once showed its character. The figure walked across the wooden floor that looked as dead as everything else. Minions were staring out from rooms and behind furniture as the figure walked past not even paying them any mind.

The figure walked down the seemingly never-ending hallway until it came to a big black door. It did not look out of place in a house that resembled death itself. Black leather covered the door with dark symbols. There was no handle, only a black crystal in the middle of the door. A cloaked arm raised as a pale hand reached out to touch the crystal. Blackness swirled within the crystal before seeping out over the hand until no whiteness could be seen. The figure stood there as calm as if it had just knocked on the door and was waiting for permission to enter. Maybe it had.

A hissing sound could be heard as the Shadows that were encasing the figure's hand retreated back into the crystal, and the door slowly opened. No sign of age or decay could be seen as the Shadow entered the dark room. A black fireplace stood roaring in the back of the room where a high-backed chair faced it. The room as dark; yet, compared to the rest of the house, it looked rejuvenated and full of life, even if it was darker than night. There was no decay on the walls or floor, and the black furniture looked as if it had just been delivered off the furniture truck.

"Is it done?" came a deep voice from the dark figure in the chair facing the black fire burning in the fireplace.

"Of course," came the lofty reply as pale hands lifted to pull back the hood of the cloak which covered her pale features. Silver hair free from the cloak flew around her face as her dull blue eyes sought the male sitting in the chair. There stood the cloaked figure the Guardians and Arions believed they had defeated.

"Why would you want to give them such a false sense of victory?"

The male bent his dark head to look at a black crystal with white and silver swirls that was in his hand. It rarely left his person. Turning the crystal over in his hand, the colors swirled inside as if competing to be seen.

"It suits me to do so," was his enigmatic answer.

"Shouldn't we be concentrating on the final battle?" The female moved closer to the chair, watching him closely.

"I am always concentrating on the final battle." His voice was very deep, and his tone was hard and unrelenting. He looked up at the female with dark eyes that were even more unyielding than his voice. "Are you questioning my methods?"

The woman, unaffected by his hard demeanor, watched him closely before replying in her soft gentle tone that belied all she stood for. "Of course not, loved one. I just don't see how giving those children any sense of accomplishment will suit our purposes."

The male's dark brow rose slightly over his right eye at her words. "Our purpose?"

The woman said nothing, but there was a modest blanch of her features that only the trained eye of the male sitting in the chair could have seen. He let out a dark chuckle knowing his words had affected the woman even if she didn't want to show it.

"You forget, woman. I am the Shadowmaster, and it is what I want that matters."

The woman's features tightened just for a moment before she relaxed and gave a slight bow of her head in respect. "Of course, my Master, but you would also do well to listen to the counsel of your most trusted advisor."

"Is that what you are?" came the smooth deep reply from the male who had turned away to once again stare into the dark flames that danced in the fireplace as if looking for an escape.

"Of course!" Her voice had a perplexed tone and if the male had been looking at her, he would have seen her eyes narrow at him. "Why would you question me on my loyalty? Wasn't it I who revealed your true power to you? Without me, you would still be nothing more than a trained pet to that female."

There was no warning of the male's movement; it was as if he was a Shadow himself as he went from sitting calmly on the chair to looming over the female, his features darker than before. Darkness rose all around him as it slithered towards the female whose eyes widened in fear.

"Yes, you revealed to me that which Lucius denied me, but do I really need you anymore?" his deep voice rasped out in his anger at her daring. The Shadows moved at his command to surrounded her and closed in so that there was no escape. "You seem to have an inflated view of your usefulness to me."

The female started to feel the air around her go stagnant, and she began to gasp for air as the Shadows began to close in. She could feel their coldness on her skin and for the first time in her life, she felt afraid of the Shadows she thought she commanded as well. She tried to beseech the Master, but no words came out; it was as if the Shadows were taking away her voice as well as the air.

"Maybe instead of giving those children a sense of false sense of victory, I give them a real one." The male's eyes darkened to the point that there was nothing but blackness. In his eyes, the female could see her reflection, her shrinking reflection.

The male turned away from her and walked towards the fireplace as the Shadows withdrew leaving the female gasping for air as she knelt on the floor. Her eyes were full of tears from the struggle of trying to breathe just moments before.

"Let the children have this victory. Let them savor the feeling that they are more powerful than they truly are." He turned to give the still kneeling female a hard look. "Let them have the illusion that they have a chance of defeating me. And when they walk into that final battle with their distorted belief that they are stronger than they are, I will show them exactly how weak they truly are."

The female's eyes widened at his words. "I'm-"

He cut her off with a raise of his hand. "Never doubt me again."

She gave a very frightened nod but said nothing.

"Leave me. There is still much I need to plan for these incredibly special children."

She looked up at his back once again, but he didn't turn nor acknowledge her hasty retreat. He just stared into the fire.

About the Author

TL Shively is an award-winning author who loves her husband and three boys; they are not only a lot of her inspiration but also her greatest supporters. She is very outnumbered in a house full of boys; even their dog is male. Her whole life has been full of stories that used to be only in her head, entertaining her when she was younger and lived in the country where the nearest neighbor was miles down the road. It wasn't until she was much older that she finally put these stories down on paper, and it was the Sanctuary Guardian's story that came out.

She loves anything fantasy: gaming, reading, writing, knick-knacks, you name it. She loves crafting of almost any kind and comes from a very artistic family.

Other books by TL Shively

The Sanctuary Guardian Series

The Independence Mine Disaster
(A short story prequel in the Sanctuary Guardian Series)

The Secret Sanctuary
(book one in the Sanctuary Guardian Series)

The Town That Time Forgot
(book two in the Sanctuary Guardian Series)